ASSAULT ON
BLACK REACH

More Warhammer 40,000 from Black Library

DARK IMPERIUM
Guy Haley

EISENHORN: XENOS
Dan Abnett

GAUNT'S GHOSTS:
THE FOUNDING OMNIBUS
Dan Abnett

CADIA STANDS
Justin D Hill

THE TALON OF HORUS
Aaron Dembski-Bowden

SIN OF DAMNATION
Gav Thorpe

CRUSADE
Andy Clark

SPACE MARINE CONQUESTS

THE DEVASTATION OF BAAL
Guy Haley

ASHES OF PROSPERO
Gav Thorpe

WAR OF SECRETS
Phil Kelly

ASSAULT ON
BLACK REACH

Nick Kyme

BLACK LIBRARY

For my battle-brothers; for Richard and Anthony.
Courage and Honour.

A BLACK LIBRARY PUBLICATION

First published in Great Britain in 2008 by
Black Library
This edition published in Great Britain in 2018 by
Black Library,
Games Workshop Ltd.,
Willow Road,
Nottingham, NG7 2WS, UK.

10 9 8 7 6 5 4 3 2 1

Produced by Games Workshop in Nottingham.
Cover illustration by David Gallagher.

A CIP record for this book is available from the British Library.

ISBN 13: 978-1-78496-747-5

See Black Library on the internet at

blacklibrary.com

Find out more about Games Workshop
and the worlds of Warhammer 40,000 at

games-workshop.com

Printed and bound by CPI Group (UK) Ltd, Croydon, CR0 4YY

It is the 41st millennium. For more than a hundred centuries the Emperor has sat immobile on the Golden Throne of Earth. He is the Master of Mankind by the will of the gods, and master of a million worlds by the might of His inexhaustible armies. He is a rotting carcass writhing invisibly with power from the Dark Age of Technology. He is the Carrion Lord of the Imperium for whom a thousand souls are sacrificed every day, so that he may never truly die.

Yet even in his deathless state, the Emperor continues His eternal vigilance. Mighty battlefleets cross the daemon-infested miasma of the warp, the only route between distant stars, their way lit by the Astronomican, the psychic manifestation of the Emperor's will. Vast armies give battle in His name on uncounted worlds. Greatest amongst His soldiers are the Adeptus Astartes, the Space Marines, bioengineered super-warriors. Their comrades in arms are legion: the Astra Militarum and countless planetary defence forces, the ever-vigilant Inquisition and the tech-priests of the Adeptus Mechanicus to name only a few. But for all their multitudes, they are barely enough to hold off the ever-present threat from aliens, heretics, mutants – and worse.

To be a man in such times is to be one amongst untold billions. It is to live in the cruellest and most bloody regime imaginable. These are the tales of those times. Forget the power of technology and science, for so much has been forgotten, never to be re-learned. Forget the promise of progress and understanding, for in the grim dark future there is only war. There is no peace amongst the stars, only an eternity of carnage and slaughter, and the laughter of thirsting gods.

PHASE ONE – BOMBARDMENT

Terrible beauty.

That was how Master Varken Mathius had described it in the fortress-monastery on Macragge, home world of the Ultramarines.

'You'll remember your first drop pod assault,' he'd said, stalking the length of the lectorium, the sound of bionics concealed beneath his mentor's robes whirring as he moved. 'Encased in a spear-tip of metal, you'll descend into a world of noise. The beat of plasma engines will resonate inside your skull, the screech of metal will tear at your resolve and the dead certainty that all which stands between you and oblivion is a thin wall of ceramite will fill your stomach like lead. The drop pod assault is a weapon of utmost swiftness and terror,' he'd told them. 'To look upon it is to behold a thing of terrible beauty.

'But you will endure it,' the master had continued. 'You will endure it because you are Astartes, the sons of Guilliman himself – there is none better amongst all your brother Chapters. You are the galaxy's finest warriors. The Ultramarines.'

Sergeant Scipio Vorolanus remembered these words well, standing in his grav-harness, the adamantium interior of his own gunmetal cocoon and nine of his battle-brothers surrounding him. Over a hundred and twenty long years had passed since that day, since he'd been a humble neophyte. He had been just a boy back then, accepting the expert tutelage of his betters, tremulous at the thought of distant battle amongst the stars. It was before the fear had been taken out of him and his rebirth through the gene-science of the Imperium into a warrior-god.

Clad in their full Astartes battle-plate, the stylised 'U' symbol depicting the allegiance of their Chapter prevalent on their armour, the warriors around Scipio stood unmoving in a circle. Nine pairs of eyes stared back at the sergeant, cold and hard behind the emerald lenses of their battle helms; superhuman beings ready for war, who gripped bolters in their armoured gauntlets like holy icons.

Only Scipio went unhooded. Better that his brothers saw the vehemence in his eyes, his devotion and courage. His close-cropped head reflected the winking operation runes inside the drop pod. The glowing symbols cast light onto the hard metal edges of the vessel interior into which the Space Marines were packed. They also displayed that the drop pod's inertial dampening system was in effect and that their rapid trajectory was being guided by its machine-spirit with unerring precision.

Thunder echoed dully from below. Scipio could hear it over the roar of the drop prod's engines as they vented. The low *crump* of detonating plasma warheads exploding planet-side was a concussive throb to the raucously disgorging thrusters. They were right on the heels of the raining plasma storm, screaming from the sky in a world of deafening noise and flashing fire.

It was a bold plan, fashioned by their liege-lord, Captain Sicarius of 2nd Company and Master of the Watch. The ork horde must be broken, and the will of the greenskins amassing on the planet below was tied to a single warlord. The bombardment would draw the beast out, and Sicarius intended his Ultramarines to be there when it did.

Slay the beast; kill the horde.

That was Sicarius's maxim, and who there would refute him save for Iulus. But then 'reckless' wasn't a word banded around lightly or obviously where the Captain of the Ultramarines 2nd Company was concerned.

The walls shuddered from the impact of re-entry, forcing Scipio's thoughts back to the present as the anguished metal screeched for his attention. The rush and roar built to a powerful crescendo. External temperature readings spiked to incredible levels as warning runes pulsed insistently.

Scipio ignored them. Instead, he opened his mouth and gave full voice to the Litany of Vengeance, leading his squad in the rites of battle, his words warring with the din inside the drop pod. As one, his warriors took up the recital and the lone voice of Scipio became a bellow of brothers. They fell fast with all the power of a comet, the prow of their drop pod white-hot and trailing fire as it burst through Black Reach's atmospheric barrier.

Scipio closed his eyes as he sang, imagining the drop pod's descent in his mind as clear as if he were actually witnessing it: the hard metal spear as it ripped through the heavens, its approach angle arrow sharp; contrails of smoke and flame peeling off the hull; a cluster of bullet-nosed vessels, lit up like fiery teardrops, surging down alongside it. The sight of those falling stars was a herald, a harbinger.

The Angels of Death are descending from on high and they are coming. They are coming for you.

They were close. Seconds to landfall. Scipio jammed on his helmet; its brow was decorated with a gilded laurel. He would justify again the weight of that honour this day, measure it in greenskin dead.

'Squad Vorolanus, make ready!' he bellowed over the shriek of the drop pod's engines as they gave their last. 'Remember who you are,' he told them. 'You are Ultramarines. You are the Emperor's finest warriors. Thunderbolts,' he said, using the squad's agnomen. 'Let us paint this day in the blood of His enemies.'

As one, Scipio's battle-brothers roared in affirmation.

'Emperor's finest,' he repeated, warning lights screaming. 'Courage and honour!'

'Courage and honour!' they cried, and the drop pod smashed into the surface of Black Reach.

As the plasma missiles continued to fall like thermo-nuclear rain, their titanic impacts vibrating through the drop pod's hull as it started to split, Scipio thought for a moment that they might have to run the gauntlet of the bombardment too. He hoped that Iulus wasn't right and that Sicarius's plan wasn't indeed reckless...

Space Marine Strike Cruiser Valin's Revenge,
two weeks earlier

'You know I'm right,' snarled Sergeant Fennion.

'I know that Sicarius is High Suzerain, that he earned honours at Crusat Minor, Dyzanyr and Fort Telendrar. That is what I know, Iulus,' hissed Sergeant Manorian in return.

Scipio had been privy to their entire hushed conversation, and knew that the debate was growing heated when Manorian reverted to calling Sergeant Fennion by his first name.

Sergeant Praxor Manorian was thin-faced with close shaven silver hair and as straight-backed as they came. Honour and glory was his chief credo, so, if Iulus was to be believed, he had much in common with his captain. Iulus, on the other hand, could not be more different. Sacrificing idealism for pragmatism, he was primarily concerned with getting the job done. He had little use for laurels and medals, though he wore his Iron Skull, the insignia for all sergeants, proudly.

Iulus's appearance matched his demeanour. He had a flat nose and a square jaw. A pepper wash of stubble was scattered over his head. His face was about as uncompromising and rigid as a Space Marine's could get. Scipio had seen rocks with more character. The bluntness extended to Iulus's voicing of opinion too; opinions that had roused the interest of others. For hushed though it was, his and Praxor's exchange had alerted the attention of their fellow sergeants.

They all sat together around a white table; it, like the icons on their power armour, was fashioned into the Ultramarine symbol. The room itself was well lit by lume-globes set in alcoves along the three walls. They threw an azure cast over everything and made the Ultramarines' blue power armour shine with even greater lustre. The fourth wall was dominated by an immense double blast door carved in ornate filigree and depicting, split over the two faces, Chapter Master Marneus Calgar seated upon the throne of Macragge, the fabled Gauntlets of Ultramar resting on his lap. The rest of the chamber sported little ornamentation. The banner of 2nd Company hung reverently upon the wall opposite the blast doors. It sat proudly behind a shimmering integrity field, refracted light from the lume-globes the only clue to the field's presence. It was a powerful totem, displaying the heraldry of the vaunted company alongside some of Captain Sicarius's very own merits.

The noble captain's entire officer cadre awaited him in the strategium, one of many in the strike cruiser. The chamber's austerity was only exacerbated by its size – there was room enough to accommodate half the 2nd Company – and sound echoed powerfully within its white walls, hence the current interest in the sergeants' thinly-veiled conversation.

'I do not deny his valour, Praxor. In that regard Sicarius is beyond reproach', snapped Iulus, and turned to face his debating partner directly. 'It is his ambition which I question, and the reckless ends to which he pursues it.'

Praxor snorted contemptuously, turning away.

'You only fear his favour will eclipse that of Agemman.'

'And is that such a ridiculous claim? Who would not wish to be at the right hand of the Chapter Master, to become the Regent of Ultramar?'

Like many organisations within the Imperium, the Ultramarines Chapter, despite being a strongly-forged brotherhood, had its factions. It functioned not unlike a republic, with Calgar as its president. In times gone by, Macragge had its battle kings, warrior-monarchs who led and governed its peoples; now it had democracy and solidarity, a republic in many respects with the sergeants within its companies as its senators. At least this was how Scipio interpreted it.

There were several positions of power within the Chapter. Highest were those of Chapter Command: Lord Calgar himself and Chaplain Ortan Cassius, his Master of Sanctity, and then the other masters. Next came the company captains and of these, two in particular vied for a seat at Marneus Calgar's right hand. Agemman held the prestige of leading 1st Company, the veterans of the Chapter and its finest warriors; Sicarius, though, was a star in the ascendant, Master of the Watch and High Suzerain of the Ultramarines. Some, the die-hard factionalists that supported Agemman, believed that the Captain of 2nd Company regarded the regent's position enviously. Iulus was one such arch-traditionalist, and it was a widely held belief that he desired to join 1st Company himself and be at the side of Agemman. Praxor Manorian, however, held a differing view and saw only Sicarius the hero, Sicarius the battle leader. Like most of the 2nd, to him the captain was above any reproach, his tactics sound and beyond question. All respected his bravery; all venerated Sicarius as they should with him as their captain.

'You are very quiet, Scipio, what do you say?'

Scipio groaned inwardly. Iulus had obviously tired of trying to convert Praxor and was turning his attentions elsewhere. Scipio, though, had no wish to join the debate. The sergeant had not long joined the 2nd and had no wish to tarnish or even endanger his future tenure by being drawn into internal politics.

Scipio regarded the faces of the officers around the table – seven sergeants, not including himself, Iulus and Praxor, five along each curve of the stylised 'U'. Young and old, scarred and unblemished, shaven-headed – all were stern of face and bore multiple service studs drilled into their skulls; one for every hundred years of service to the Chapter.

The seated sergeants returned Scipio's gaze stoically; some nodding in fraternal camaraderie, others just meeting it with steel in their eyes. One such sergeant was Arcus Helios. He was not of the 2nd; he was one of Agemman's chosen, a veteran whose usual attire was the tactical dreadnought armour of the Terminators. He eschewed that suit of tank-busting, nigh-on indestructibility for his power armour now; the former being a highly impractical choice, even given the expansive strategium. If Helios had heard any of the debate between the other two sergeants and thought anything of it, he did not show it.

There was another not of 2nd Company within the room, and Scipio's gaze strayed to him next. He stayed in the shadows at the edge of the chamber, just beyond the glow of the lume-globes. Though shrouded in gloom, Scipio's enhanced vision made out a face framed by a grey-white beard, with patrician cheekbones. A long camo-cloak hung over the warrior's broad shoulders which were bereft of the power-armoured pauldrons worn by every other officer in the room.

Scipio had not noticed him before. Perhaps he had wished not to be noticed. He perched – for he seemed in such a state of idle readiness that it could hardly be called 'standing' – in absolute stillness, so inert that Scipio might have mistaken him for a statue. This then was Telion, Brother-Sergeant of the 10th, master scout, a veteran under three different Chapter Masters and battle-tutor to four of the current Ultramarines' captains. There were not enough honours and service studs crafted by the Chapter artisans to fit *his* brow and breast.

Telion returned the young sergeant's gaze, and his eyes were like ice. Scipio looked away despite himself.

'Well?' Iulus pressed.

In his desire to break visual contact with the intimidating Telion, Scipio's eyes fell upon a final figure. Armoured in black ceramite replete with icons of death and mortality, this one stood alone, and he was no less threatening.

'We are blessed to have two such noble heroes in our midst,' Scipio replied at last, mustering some diplomacy. 'And I also think that Chaplain Orad would take a dim view of this debate.'

Iulus had clearly followed his gaze, and stayed silent before the glowering countenance of the Chaplain. Orad had been attached to 2nd Company for many long years. None amongst the battle-brothers could ever recall him removing his skull-mask battle helm, at least not in public. Rumours abounded that most his face had been burned off, eaten away by bio-acid, fighting the tyranid of Hive Fleet Behemoth over a hundred years ago. Apocryphal or not, the very fact that the Chaplain effectively had a bleached skull for a head compounded his already fearsome reputation. He spoke in a harsh, grating whisper, his voice enhanced by a vox-unit built into his gorget that made it audible and metallic. Yes, Orad was every inch the forbidding spectre.

The silence that fell at last was short-lived. The mighty blast doors to the strategium split open and slid apart, and a wash of warm ochre light spilled in from the corridor beyond. Shadows were immediately realised in the pool of spreading light, long and low as they reached into the room. Sicarius's command squad, the Lions of Macragge, stepped in, and the officer cadre stood as one, turning to face them.

First into the room was Daceus, a veteran sergeant who had fought with the captain in every one of his campaigns. He'd lost an eye at the Siege of Zalathras, and the bionic replacement whirred and clicked as it surveyed the standing officers. Brothers Prabian and Vandius followed, Prabian wore his power sword and combat shield attached to his belt, while Vandius glanced at the company banner that he usually carried, and muttered an oath of piety. Last were Venatio, Apothecary to the 2nd, and Brother Malcian. These Astartes were heroes all, their bravery filling the Chapter's archives for many volumes. But even combined they could not hope to match the valour of the one who strode in next.

Upright and imperious, head held high, he seemed to glow with inner glory. He was resplendent in his artificer armour, crafted by the Chapter artisans upon his appointment to High Suzerain. He cradled an ornate battle helm in the crook of his arm, the low crest running from left to right temple an indication of his superiority and rank. An array of pteruges hung beneath a broad loincloth dedicated with the stylised symbol of the Chapter, and the armoured plastron he wore over his chest was wreathed with honour brocade.

Cato Sicarius had entered the chamber, and all within it, even the cantankerous Iulus, could not help but be lifted by his presence. Master of the Watch, High Suzerain of Ultramar, Knight Champion of

Macragge, Grand Duke Talassar: Sicarius had many titles, all earned on the battlefield, all dispensed for the glory of his many great deeds and victories. But in truth, he valued only one: captain.

Sicarius strode into the strategium, eyeing each of his officers in turn and giving a slight nod to Arcus Helios to acknowledge him as a battle-brother from a company other than the 2nd. Chaplain Orad followed his captain, and the Lions of Macragge fell into line behind him. When Sicarius came to the apex of the U-shaped strategium table, he stood in the void where the two points of the sweeping arc ended, and started speaking.

'Welcome, brothers.' His voice was noble, but filled with inner steel and undeniable confidence. 'Please. Sit,' he told them, and the officers obeyed. The Lions joined them at the tips of the U, occupying the last of the empty positions. Only Orad and the captain himself remained standing. Scipio noticed that Telion also remained where he was, and showed no visible sign of deference. But something had passed between the veteran scout and Sicarius. In his marrow, Scipio felt it. Respect.

'We are two weeks from the Black Reach system,' Sicarius began, once his officers were reseated. 'Immortal renown for the 2nd, the Guardians of the Temple, awaits us there.'

Scipio felt Iulus stiffen slightly at the captain's apparent vainglory.

'Daceus,' the captain added, nodding to his battle-brother.

The veteran sergeant rose to his feet and saluted,

before activating a series of runic icons on the face of the strategium table. In the central point of the plate floor, delineated by the U, a hololith flickered into life, depicting a revolving green orb. The planet had several landmasses and was riddled with thick water tributaries, like fat through marbled beef, running from several major oceans. A wreath of smaller objects, a dense asteroid belt, swarmed around it, occasionally obscuring the view.

'The planet of Black Reach, principle world of the Black Reach sector,' Daceus announced. 'A mining world, Black Reach has little obvious value to Ultramar yet it is tactically crucial,' he explained.

The sergeant pressed another rune on the sunken panel set into the table. The planetary image zoomed out, displaying the entire sector. 'Jede'ogh and Voldermacht,' he said, indicating two further worlds that had been revealed in the image shift. The immense asteroid field swathed all three. 'And here,' Daceus added, scrolling the image to one side with a desultory sweep of his gauntlet.

A roiling mass of warp space, a rift in the layer of reality, was revealed circulating at the fringe of the sector. To Scipio it looked like a baleful eye, ragged and torn, seething with incandescent energy. Despite its pseudo-incorporeal form, it was visible even through the grainy resolution of the holo-capture.

'Jorgund's Eye,' Daceus named it. 'Through this wyrmhole a massive horde of greenskins has descended on Black Reach. It is unknown to us how such a thing was possible, how the ork could have caught us by surprise. It matters not. The facts are these: the greenskins have invaded the system and even now wage war upon the planet of Black Reach. Should their assault prove successful, the aliens will have gained a foothold in such close proximity to Ultramar as to make the Chapter Master nervous. Furthermore, the asteroid belt surrounding the system contains high concentrations of magnetic ore, making long-range augur probes all-but impossible.'

'We cannot afford to let the greenskin infect this sector,' Sicarius continued for his veteran sergeant. 'I for one have no desire to engage in a lengthy purging campaign of the planets and all their astral bodies. Such an enterprise is costly. It would take us centuries to exterminate the alien scum if they were allowed to carry on unchecked. There is no honour in that.'

Scipio felt Iulus bristle again, but he ignored him. By contrast, Praxor was utterly enrapt by the captain's words.

'Like any horde,' Sicarius continued, 'remove the head and the body will die.'

He smiled grimly. 'The orks have a head. A warlord, who, we have learned by vox-monitoring the Imperial planetary communications below, goes by the name of Zanzag. This creature must die. I will not rest until its head is mounted on a spike. *My* spike.' Sicarius nodded to Daceus for him to continue.

'Finding the ork warlord will not be easy,' said the veteran sergeant. 'If reports from the surface are to be believed, the beast has engaged in a series of lightning raids that has left nine of the original twelve hive cities in ruins, taken by the greenskins. Such inexplicable cunning is uncharacteristic for the ork, and we have yet to determine how such an assault was even possible.'

'The orks have laid waste to this world, but it stops here. Now,' Sicarius declared. 'We will go in swift and hard, via drop pod assault. Prior to our insertion, the *Valin's Revenge* will bombard the planet from orbit, launching plasma torpedoes into the greenskin forces. We will come in the wake of the ordnance, like hellhounds on the heels of its fiery wrath.' He grinned ferally. 'Wherever the orks stand and fight, we will strike hardest. For there we will find our quarry.'

'Launching such an attack directly behind a planetary bombardment – the risks are incredible,' said Iulus, unable to keep his discontent in check any longer.

'I agree with Sergeant Fennion,' said another dissenting voice, Sergeant Solinus of the Indomitable. He was the battle leader of the vaunted warriors who took Fort Telendrar. They were the first Astartes into the breach after Captain Sicarius, a feat that had earned them the Victorex Maxima. 'Is such a strategy even feasible?'

Daceus was about to intervene, when Sicarius raised a hand to stop him.

'Brothers,' the captain replied, spreading his arms in a gesture of solidarity. 'For us,' he shook his head, giving a belligerent smile, 'nothing is impossible. A swift assault will catch the enemy off guard. Kill the head, and the body will die,' he repeated. 'Our victory will be assured. We are 2nd Company. We are the slayers of kings, the destroyers of worlds, bringers of death and ruination in all its forms. These things we do in the name of the Emperor and in the defence of mankind. I say let none stay our wrath.'

Scipio could not help but feel the pride in his captain's voice and knew the entire officer cadre felt it too.

Praxor nodded with vehemence, smacking his fist against the cuirass of his power armour in affirmation and salute. The other officers followed his example, even Sergeant Solinus. Iulus was last of all, and gave a single firm rap against his armour. Sicarius held the truculent sergeant's gaze for a moment before he moved on.

'Is there anything further?' he asked.

'What Imperial forces can we expect to find on the planet surface?' replied Sergeant Atavian of the Titan Slayers. The Devastator squad battle leader growled the words. A long scar ran down the left side of his face and terminated in a bionic eye, which added to his grim appearance.

It was Daceus who answered. 'Black Reach has its own Imperial Guard garrison, the Sable Gunners. They are well stretched across the four continents of the world, marshalling its hive cities and the numerous aqueducts that feed its reservoirs. Strategium indicates that the beleaguered defenders have been fighting the orks for two months, local time. Morale will be low, and casualties high. As such, any aid from that quarter will be negligible.'

'And the greenskins,' added Iulus. 'What are our estimations of their forces?'

'The ork are concentrated on the northern continent.' Daceus gestured with his gauntlet again, and the hololith zoomed in at a rapid rate of magnification. A large landmass was revealed, surrounded by black tributaries, with two towering spikes that were hives. 'Their main offensive is dedicated to sacking Ghospora,' he explained, pointing out the largest of the two hive cities displayed on the hololith. 'We reckon their numbers to be in the region of fifty thousand, well spread out, with armour and heavy artillery.'

'Against one hundred,' stated Iulus.

'Good odds, brother-sergeant,' Captain Sicarius intervened.

'Indeed, brother-captain,' Iulus replied, levelly.

The captain smiled back at him without mirth, and nodded. 'If there is nothing more...' Sicarius turned to his veteran sergeant.

'We begin planetfall here,' said Daceus, 'at the north wall of Ghospora.'

Black Reach, northern continent, Ghospora Hive City, two weeks later

Pale light limned the interior of the drop pod. The doors slammed open seconds later as the vessel opened like a gunmetal bloom, venting steam, its hull still smouldering. The ochre sands of Black Reach had been scorched to glass with the intense heat radiation of the drop pod's arrival. It crunched underfoot as Scipio and his nine Astartes came out, bolters singing.

The drop pod's deathwind missile launcher armaments jolted with explosive recoil, a percussive chorus to the steady throb of bolter fire. A kill-zone of slain orks was forged around the landing site in seconds from the punitive barrage.

It bought a few moments' grace for Scipio to see the cauldron of battle.

They had descended into the eye of the storm. Ahead of them, some five hundred metres or more, the north wall of Ghospora Hive loomed like a black bulkhead cliff. It was some eight kilometres across and stretched eighty kilometres high into Black Reach's pollutant-laden upper atmosphere. Gunports, bunkers and battle-towers bristling with cannon and long-range sensor arrays hugged the extremities of the hive city like space debris clinging to the hull of a dead starship. Smoke billowed from the wrecked defences and fires raged unchecked along partially destroyed sections of the outer bastion wall. It was here at the forefront of the greenskin assault where the Imperial Guard Sable Gunners were making their last stand. Scipio's enhanced vision, cycling through its various filters to ascertain the optimum visual spectrum, and augmented by the technology within his battle helm, detected the heat signatures from several heavy weapon emplacements.

The native soldiery of Black Reach were dug in around bunkers and entrenchments crested with razor wire. Even from a distance, Scipio could tell it was a thin line. Officers barked orders down the length of the fracturing wall, charred banners rose and fell. Men died in their droves.

A veritable sea of greenskins surrounded them, stretching for kilometres across and back in a dark mass. The thrashing ocean of aliens lapped at the meagre bulwarks of Ghospora Hive, threatening to overwhelm them. Ramshackle battle tanks and crudely-fashioned trucks festooned with cannon, rockets and other ordnance bounded madly alongside thronging mobs of green-skinned orks, decked in thick battle armour hammered with additional metal plates and daubed in crude glyphs. Diminutive gretchin capered in the wake of their larger cousins, swathed in little more than rags, brandishing over-sized pistols or scraps of battlefield debris to use as improvised weapons.

Hulking mechanical constructs, the bastardised greenskin equivalent of Space Marine dreadnoughts, lumbered in the midst of the horde in clusters, rending with claws and razor-saws or loosing staccato bursts of automatic fire and errant missile salvos.

Though broken up and battered from the strike cruiser bombardment – with thousands slain in the initial barrage, and some fleeing in terror or cowering beneath what little battlefield cover there was – it was still a vast horde. And it stood between Scipio and his objective.

'Thunderbolts form up on me, fire-pattern *omega*,' he said, unleashing his bolt pistol's wrath into the rearguard of the greenskin ranks as the Space Marines started to move forwards. A splinter of the horde, now evidently aware of the Ultramarines' arrival, had broken off from the rest and swarmed towards the drop pods.

Orks were huge, slab-muscled monsters. Sloping brows and broad chins, jutting with thick yellow tusks, gave them a distinctly porcine appearance. They were beasts, and lived only for battle. Survival of the strongest was their only creed, and one they demonstrated to brutal effect.

Scipio formed the tip of a spear, as his battle-brothers moved into formation around him. At one flank, Brother Garrik braced his missile launcher. Dropping to one knee for stability, he fired. A heavy *whoosh* of expelling incendiary blasted over Scipio's head and an ork truck careening towards the squad was immolated in a ball of flame.

'One for the Thunderbolts!' yelled Garrik, his voice grainy through the comm-feed of Scipio's helmet.

The conflagration spread, belching oily smoke and devouring any orks and gretchin in its path, but the greenskin splinter mob was undeterred.

Scipio's bolt pistol jolted in his armoured grasp, exploding apart an onrushing ork's skull. The beast ran on headless for a few more seconds in a macabre display of tenacity before it slumped and fell.

A gout of promethium spewed from Brother Hekor's flamer on the right flank, engulfing a swathe of belligerent greenskins. Some barrelled on through the intense heat, their bodies alight. Bursts of sporadic but controlled bolter fire put them down before they could get close.

At the edge of his peripheral vision, Scipio saw other squads moving up alongside him, adopting similar assault formations as they made their approach. But this was just an advance force, fighting an initial sortie to secure the landing zone and gain a foothold on the killing field – the real battle was still to come.

Several war-bikes and thickly armoured buggies bounced along with the splinter mob, belt-fed heavy cannons barking, ammo cases cascading like brass rain onto their flatbeds. The motorcade of green-skin vehicles picked up speed, smoke gushing from exhausts, spits of flame bursting from the over-charged engines.

A whistling contrail from a krak missile weaved over Scipio's shoulder and took out one of the bug-gies, blasting apart its front axle and upending the machine onto its roof. The roll-bar capitulated instantly, crushing the goggled driver and the orks on the flatbed. A rolling firestorm then engulfed the buggy and its crew as the fuel canister went up and burned them all to ash.

Scipio commended Brother Garrik for his fine shooting over the comm-feed.

Further explosions rippled down the makeshift ork line as bikes and buggies were ripped apart by bursts of heavy bolter fire or skewered on lances of las or blasts of promethium.

Extending a chopping arm, Scipio took out one of the bikers as it sped past him. He felt the greenskin's neck snap as he made contact. The bike slewed into a skid, ramming into another and the two vehicles exploded together in a fiery wreck.

The motorised vanguard was down. The Ultramarines' squads had been efficient in its destruction and were yet to take a casualty. Now they'd meet the splinter horde up close.

Through the carnage, solid shot pranging off his pauldrons and greaves as the orks sought to retaliate against the Astartes' fire superiority, Scipio saw the mob leader.

The massive brute bellowed at its warriors, spittle flying from its maw. Crudely stitched scars laced its face like patchwork, and metal rings and bones punctured the thick flesh of its ears, lips and brow. It wore a fur-trimmed helmet, crested by a pair of horns. An interlocking hauberk of riveted iron plates bulged with the musculature of its immense body.

The beast howled with rage as it charged at Scipio, brandishing a blood-slicked cleaver in challenge and squeezing off desultory rounds from a fat pistol. More greenskins flanked it, some pitched from their feet or staggered by bolter fire as the rest of the Thunderbolts tried to slay them from a distance. The brutish creatures bellowed in exultation of the fight to come. They wouldn't have to wait long.

Scipio thumbed the activation rune of his chainsword, and with a throaty roar the weapon churned to life.

'For Sicarius and the primarch!' he cried, and prepared to meet his foe.

As they closed, Scipio held his bolt pistol's trigger down. The muzzle-flare lit up the ork's snarling face as a tracery of rounds ripped up its shoulder.

The beast was barely slowed. It shrugged off the wound and smacked Scipio's pistol aside before he could fire again. The ork mob leader then drove its cleaver downward, hoping to shatter Scipio's clavicle beneath his power armour. But the sergeant parried the blow with his chainsword, the serrated teeth spitting sparks as they ground against metal. Blades locked together, the ork pressed its weight against the blow, and Scipio felt his legs starting to buckle. He swept his bolt pistol around again, but the ork caught his wrist and held it fast. Explosive rounds barked off ineffectually to one side, chewing up sand. Bearing down on him, the ork's face twisted in what Scipio assumed was a grin. Its beady red eyes, sunken beneath its overhanging brow, glittered with malice.

In his armour, Scipio stood almost two and a half metres tall, yet he was still dwarfed by the huge greenskin. Superhuman muscles flexing with every shred of strength he could muster, Scipio pushed back. The servos in his power armour whined with effort. He was so close to the beast's leering face that he could smell the stink of its vile breath even through his helmet's atmospheric filters.

'What are you smiling at, ugly?' he snarled through gritted teeth and smashed a brutal head butt into the ork's snout. Dark blood gushed from its ruptured nose and the ork squealed in anger and pain.

There was a momentary lift of pressure. Scipio exploited it to the full. He heaved, pushed with his legs and arms simultaneously, and threw the greenskin off. The beast was unbalanced for a second, more than long enough for Scipio to ram the churning blade of his chainsword into its gut. Penetrating armour plate, he twisted and turned the weapon in search of vital organs, while the ork thrashed and bucked on the end of it like a stuck pig. Still it fought, and was about to swing its cleaver again when Scipio brought up his bolt pistol, rammed the muzzle in the greenskin's screaming maw and pulled the trigger. The ork's brain pan punched out of the back of its head, amidst a shower of gore and skull fragments, and at last it was dead. Scipio ripped his chainsword free, deactivating it before release so as not to spit chunks of viscera over his battle-brothers, and made a rapid tactical assessment of the battlefield.

The greenskin rearguard was vanquished. Even now Ultramarines squads moved in staggered battle formations to close the gap between the remnants of the ork rear echelon and the main horde beyond.

The landing site was secure. Devastator squads bearing the majority of the Astartes heavy firepower took up position at the back on the quickly established Ultramarines battle-line. They advanced slowly behind the tactical squad vanguard, two of which had converged on the Thunderbolts' position in order to form one flank of the Space Marine battle group. Scipio recognised the squad markings of Iulus and Praxor at once, the Immortals and the Shield Bearers.

'Rough deployment, Iulus?' Scipio remarked through the comm-feed of his battle helm.

Iulus's drop pod had crash landed, three of its exit ramps incapacitated as it had dug itself into a sand bank and held fast. The sergeant's armour was scorched from the fire that had obviously ensued, as was the armour of his squad as they moved to the Thunderbolts' right.

'Plasma detonation clipped us,' he snapped. 'Got caught in its blast wave. I told you this plan was reckless–'

'You're alive, aren't you?' countered Praxor, his own squad forging up on Scipio's left.

Iulus fed a burst of static through the feed, and Scipio winced against the auditory assault.

'We have our answer,' said Praxor, adding, 'On my lead, brothers.'

Squad Moranion, the Shield Bearers, was the most experienced of the group, having been the vanguard of numerous Chapter-level assaults, and both Scipio and Iulus deferred to Praxor.

'Sergeants Tirian and Atavian assure me they're making us a gap,' he continued, the three squads advancing at pace across the scorched earth. The last few torpedoes of the bombardment erupted deep inside the ork lines as they moved, shaking the earth beneath their booted feet.

Secondary eruptions came from behind them as the two devastator squads Praxor had mentioned spat torrents of heavy fire. Beams of las and plasma, melta-flare, heavy bolter fire and spiralling missiles streaked overhead. The barrage withered one section of the greenskin line, trucks erupting in explosive blossoms. Swathes of orks shredded and burned in the vicious fusillade.

With the landing site anchored by heavy weaponry, the objective of the more mobile tactical squads was to cut a wedge through the ork horde and reach the embattled Sable Gunner regiments behind it. With the solid defences of Ghospora at their backs, the Ultramarines would have an excellent staging point at which to launch a counter offensive, retake the walls and from there lift the siege. The task of locating the ork warlord, Zanzag, fell to Sicarius, and to him alone.

As if his thoughts had heralded it, Scipio looked skyward. The armoured hull of a Thunderhawk hove into view, descending through billowing plumes of smoke, grey tendrils clinging to its sweeping wings. Dust and ash clouds scudded across the umber plain as it closed, disturbed by the down-thrust of the gunship's massive engines.

Scipio recognised the vessel's markings as its landing beams strafed the ground.

It was the *Gladius*, so-named for the short blade wielded by the Ultramarines' honour guard.

The vessel surged forward like a sword, cutting right into the heart of the greenskins massing at the north wall. Ork bodies were tossed into the air in the violent backwash of descent thrusters, crushed beneath slowly extending landing stanchions or hosed with sprays of fire from the Thunderhawk's heavy bolters.

Within seconds of coming to rest a hundred metres from the Ultramarines' swiftly advancing battle-line, the embarkation ramp was down and then there *he* was.

Sicarius.

PHASE TWO –
THE STORMING OF GHOSPORA

Cato Sicarius stormed out of the *Gladius* like Invictus reborn, hero of the first Tyrannic War, cloak flaring with the plasma winds kicked up in the wake of the bombardment.

He held aloft his power sword, the Talassarian Tempest Blade, and waded into the greenskin horde. Behind him a force disgorged from the belly of the Thunderhawk gunship. The Lions of Macragge fell upon the orks with fury, screaming the primarch's name as Sicarius pressed his relentless assault. Arcus Helios led a phalanx of Terminators that drove indomitably into the ork ranks, storm bolters roaring. Squad Solinus followed them, the heroes of Telendrar forging a bloody path with bolter and blade. Finally there came Brother Ultracius, looming over all.

Having fallen on the battlefields of Pyra over a thousand years ago, Ultracius was now entombed in the cryo-sarcophagus of a dreadnought. The battle-brother was, in effect, a massive armoured war machine. It was no battle-suit Ultracius wore, nor a form of ablative armature; it was *part* of him. In this symbiosis of flesh and machine, the battle-brother dwelled in amniotic slumber within the dreadnought's sarcophagus until it was called to war. One could not exist without the other. Man and metal were one.

Adamantium plate reinforced with fire-retardant ceramite bulked out an immense servo-driven frame, which was over five metres tall. The dreadnought's brutal weapon mounts and ancillary combat systems could be tailored to a particular engagement prior to battlefield deployment. Stylised Ultramarines iconography bolted onto his armoured carapace declared his allegiance boldly.

Ribbed cables spanned Ultracius's thick mechanical legs and arm mounts, providing the power to drive them. They hummed belligerently, the sound an extension of Ultracius's own warrior wrath, as he stomped down the gunship's embarkation ramp.

Assault cannon whirring, the dreadnought scythed down greenskins with brutal efficiency. Brother Ultracius was a symbol, an immortal warrior of the Ultramarines destined to battle on in the name of the Chapter forever.

With Sicarius at their head, no ork horde could resist them.

'All Ultramarines... advance!' he roared into the comm-feed. 'This day we see glory or death.'

The Thunderhawk assault force cleaved through the greenskin masses like a burning blade.

The captain's voice inside his battle helm stirred Scipio to greater efforts.

'Forward!' he cried, in unison with Praxor. The three squads broke into a run. Pounding across the bloody sand, leaping over the tangled remains of greenskins slain in the bombardment, the rest of the Ultramarines smashed into the orks with righteous fury.

Scipio's chainsword roared into life again, and, slamming a fresh clip into his bolt pistol, he struck as one with his battle-brothers. The deadly press was incredible. Scipio charged an ork to the ground with his shoulder before dispatching it with his chainsword. His blade still whirring in its cranium, he blasted apart the torso of another with his bolt pistol. The greenskin was biting a grenade between its teeth in some kind of kamikaze attack. As it fell, the grenade exploded taking three of the ork's kin with it.

Scipio felt the heat radiation wash against his helmet. Temperature readings spiked for an instant then fell to normal again. He and his squad strode on through the dying firestorm, finding fresh enemy to engage as they killed in the name of the Chapter.

Scipio looked right as he forged towards his next target, and saw Iulus and his squad emerging through a shower of earth and shrapnel as an ork wagon exploded nearby.

Overhead, Scipio heard the whip-spin of rotor blades. Shots were pinging off his armour as he took apart another greenskin and looked up. A rough squadron of copter-like ork attack craft buzzed into view, belching missiles. The single passenger vehicles flew in an erratic trajectory, thick smoke issuing from chugging engines. One of the machines broke off from formation, sweeping low over the Astartes ranks before it dropped an immense bomb that had been lashed to its undercarriage. Bolter fire from Squad Octavian punctured its fuel reserve and the copter exploded in mid-air, spitting debris.

Brother Castor – Scipio remembered him from their training in the scholar-houses – threw himself over the deadly ordnance to protect his fellow squad members.

A second later, the bomb detonated.

Scipio was flattened by an immense blast wave, his helmet lenses dampening the magnesium-bright after- flare. Despite this act of outrageous heroism, battle-brothers from Castor's squad were flung outward from the terrible explosion. A fat mushroom cloud billowed up in its wake, and the Space Marines crashed down to the earth hard, swathed in dust and debris. Castor was immolated, his ragged body thrown up and buoyed by the blast wave, before spiralling down into a broken heap.

Another for Apothecary Venatio, thought Scipio bitterly as Brother Hekor helped him up.

The battle still raged above, though now Assault Squads Strabo and Ixion, jump packs screaming, soared to meet the ork death-copters head-on and took them apart in a punishing hail of bolter fire and promethium. The vile engines fell like wounded fireflies into the packed greenskins, their explosive death throes wreaking still further havoc in their own ranks.

With a nod of acknowledgement to Hekor, Scipio led his squad on.

'Right flank tactical squads,' a grit-gravel voice barked through the comm-feed. There could be no mistaking the iron-hard timbre of Chaplain Orad.

'Converge on Secondary Command,' ordered the Chaplain. 'We go in support of Captain Sicarius.'

Through the melee of blades, bolts and bullets, the smoke-drenched sky lit by sporadic explosions and the staccato flash of muzzle-flares, Scipio saw the black power amour of Orad up ahead.

Orders delivered, the fearsome Chaplain spat litanies of hate and vengeance into the comm-feed on a battle group-wide frequency, urging the Ultramarines to smite the foe with extreme prejudice. His rosarius field flickered as ork bullets peppered it and fell away without causing harm. Striding into the heart of the horde, dispatching wounded greenskins with indiscriminate blasts of his plasma pistol, whilst cracking the skulls of the more able-bodied with his crackling crozius mace, the 2nd Company Chaplain was like a force of nature.

Scipio could see the lay of the unfolding battle. Sicarius had almost reached the outer bastion wall. Primary Command – consisting of the captain's retinue, the Terminators, Squad Solinus and Brother Ultracius – were engaged in fierce fighting with the most battle-hardened of the ork mobs. The warlord could not be far.

Chaplain Orad, given overall command of the

remaining ground forces, led a second group with Squads Vandar and the remnants of Octavian. Scipio's own battle group, with Iulus and Praxor, was only a hundred metres away. The devastator squads behind them advanced as a rearguard, whilst the assault squads gave lightning support wherever it was needed.

The Ultramarines controlled the field. This was the final push to the walls.

'On my lead, sergeants,' Praxor said through the comm-feed, closing the distance to Chaplain Orad on the left and slaying any greenskins that got in his way.

Scipio followed, hacking a bloody swathe through the foe, with Iulus on his rear.

A row of makeshift ork earthworks loomed ahead, death-pits and dense spirals of razor wire patrolled by cannon-toting battlewagons brimming with greenskins, and heavily-armed trucks acting as outriders. It stood between the three squads and Chaplain Orad.

'A killing field,' grunted Iulus through his battle helm, the rending sound of his chainsword muffling the words.

Scipio saw that Praxor, just ahead of them, had brought up his squad's melta gun. Iulus had done the same.

'Brother Hekor,' he said, bolt pistol roaring in his grasp, 'flamer forward.'

Praxor and Iulus would take out the armour; Scipio would burn the rest. Promethium expelled from a flamer at close range was incredibly hot, hot enough to turn the ork razor wire into molten slag. Still, the fortifications would be hard to crack.

'Where is Brother Telion when you need him, eh?' laughed Iulus, dispatching another greenskin.

'I saw no sign of him in the muster, perhaps–'

A huge explosion lit up the ork earthworks before Scipio could finish. One of the battlewagons went up, leaping spectacularly into the air before crashing down on a second vehicle, crushing it. Chained detonations followed, ripping up the death-pits and razor wire, blowing the trucks to smithereens.

'He's here,' said Praxor knowingly and bellowed, 'Space Marines, attack!'

The three squads barrelled towards the breach, cutting down the disorientated orks swarming off it with barks of bolter fire and flashing blades.

Out of the carnage appeared Telion. Unhooded, the brother-sergeant stalked amongst the panicked greenskin ranks like a true predator. No battle cries came from his lips. He was stern and cold, killing swiftly and efficiently. A four-man scout squad followed his lead. Inexplicably, they had managed to emerge in the midst of the entrenchments, having somehow found a clandestine route through the rugged battlefield landscape to approach the orks unnoticed until choosing to act.

A few metres from the attack, a Storm-pattern land speeder hovered up and away, launching a salvo of frag grenades into the clustered ork forces to safeguard its rapid ascent.

By the time Scipio and his brother-sergeants had reached the devastated ork fortifications, Telion and

his scouts were gone, drifting off like ghosts to some
other part of the battlefield. Doubtless he too was
moving in support of Sicarius.

A missile-strike from Brother Garrik widened the
gaping wreckage of the earthworks. Scipio and the
rest of the squad sped through it, Iulus and Praxor
surging through other breaches in the battered
defences.

Emerging through the smoke and dust, a metal
monstrosity filled Scipio's vision as a second wave
of ork armour moved to impede them. The machine
lumbered on thick, piston-pumping legs. A steel
torso, not unlike a metal can riveted with ork
glyph-plates and additional slabs of armour, swayed
back and forth as the machine stomped towards
them. An exhaust stuck out of its back like a spine,
chugging acrid fumes. It was nestled alongside a
crudely fashioned banner strung with bleached
human skulls.

The ork dreadnought, a five-metre-high monstrosity, was festooned with weapons: a high-calibre
cannon was bolted to its hip, a generous ammo
feed trailing to the ground from its auto-loader; two
long, hydraulic arms ended in a snapping power claw
and a rotator-saw respectively. A green targeting eye
whirred and clicked along the dreadnought's thin
vision-slit, through which Scipio detected the belligerent presence of a greenskin hard-wired into the
machine itself.

It was not alone. A second machine stomped into
view, cannon shuddering with recoil.

The rounds tore up the earth next to Scipio's feet,

but failed to find a target. A missile streaked overhead in retaliation and blew off the dreadnought's cannon as well as most of its left side. Scipio saw the greenskin pilot through the cracked metal armour of its cockpit. It juddered and shook, the wires poking out of its plated skull sparking and on fire as the neural link to its dying machine was severed.

Its partner came on undeterred, advancing over the stricken ork pilot as it continued to spasm, crushing it to paste.

Suppressing bolter fire flicked off the ork dreadnought's armoured hull, no more a deterrent than a stinging insect, as it swept its cannon around in a wide arc. Two of Scipio's battle-brothers went down in a fusillade of high-calibre bullets. The sergeant himself took a shot in the pauldron and felt it bite.

Hekor doused the ork fighting machine with promethium from his flamer. The thing caught alight briefly before the fire died and it smashed the Ultramarine aside with its massive arm. Hekor lay prone on the ground, a wide crack in his ceramite plastron oozing blood.

The other two squads were faring no better as more ork dreadnoughts, and some smaller machineries of a similar crude design, joined the fray. Scipio saw one melted down by Iulus's squad, another blown apart in his peripheral vision with krak grenades by Praxor's Shield Bearers.

Right now, though, Scipio had his own problems.

'Garrik, take it down!' he cried, as the dreadnought came at them.

'On your order, sir–*arrggh!*' The battle-brother fell, a barrage of high-calibre shells tearing up his power armour and laying him flat. Brother Brakkius went to haul him out of harm's way but was picked off by a flame-thrower attachment on the dreadnought's main cannon. Tossed around one-eighty degrees, he collapsed into a smouldering heap.

Scipio gritted his teeth, eyed up the mechanical monster and charged.

First ducking another flame-thrower burst, he then weaved under a casual sweep of the dreadnought's rotator-saw, though it caught the sergeant's banner pole affixed to his back and cut it in half. Scipio replied with a swipe of his chainsword, ripping through a bunch of hydraulic cables that fed power to the rotator-saw. The weapon screeched at first, juddering as its servos protested, but then hummed back into life.

The bolter fire had barely dented its armoured trunk-like body and Scipio searched for any advantage. He hacked the barrel off the dreadnought's stuttering cannon as it swung round, but the chain teeth got stuck three-quarters through the metal, and the weapon was wrenched away. He tried his bolt pistol again, aiming for any weak points, but tossed it away when the dreadnought brought its rotator-saw down in a punishing arc. Scipio caught it two-handed. The impact resonated all the way down his arms and into his shoulders. The spinning blade was stalled just centimetres from his battle helm.

Muscles bunching, Scipio's secondary heart kicked

in and pumped blood more rapidly around his system in order to cope with the sustained exertion. Even though the severed hydraulic cable limited the dreadnought's power, Scipio still felt his body being ground down slowly in the dirt. The rotator-saw was just millimetres from his helmet. He slipped and the blade chewed into the metal, spitting sparks. The left lens of Scipio's battle helm clouded with static as the visual feed was cut. A second more and the battle helm disintegrated around his face. Scipio shrugged away the wrecked helm as the greater movement afforded by its absence allowed him to lean back a few more vital millimetres.

The battle din, the sights and smells of the bloodied field washed over Scipio in a wave as he was stripped of his broken helmet and its sophisticated filtration systems. The sensory disorientation was only momentary; his superhuman Astartes physiology compensated at once.

The adjustment didn't help him in his current predicament. Scipio roared as the rotator-saw edged a little closer, determined to meet his end with defiance in his heart and the name of the Chapter on his lips.

'Ultramarines!' he cried, and felt a flash of intense heat against his bare face as the dreadnought was smashed aside. Rolling away from the machine and up into a battle-crouch, Scipio saw the dreadnought explode with a gaping hole of dissolved metal in its torso. Its legs crumpled and it fell into a smoking ruin.

'*Rise, Brother Vorolanus.*'

Scipio turned at the booming, automated voice and saw the imperious form of Brother Agnathio.

The Space Marine dreadnought cast a huge shadow as it towered over his fellow Astartes. The mortally-wounded battle-brother entombed within its armoured sepulchre had been stirred into sentience when the final approach to Black Reach had begun. He was a Chapter relic, interred within his dreadnought sarcophagus over five thousand years ago at the Fall of Chundrabad. The war machine's adamantium hull was girded by ornate layers of ceramite and emblazoned with the stylised iconography of the Ultramarines, all wrought by the Chapter's artificers. Reliquaries were mounted on Agnathio's broad machine shoulders, containing the bones of other noble warriors secured in micro-stasis fields. Purity seals and sheaves of parchment inscribed with oaths and litanies swathed his armoured form like holy vestments.

The venerable dreadnought twisted its torso around and fired a second pulsating beam from its multi-melta. Another of the ork machines was torn apart in a blistering explosion.

'*Only in death, does duty end.*' Agnathio's voice, fed through the vox-coder built into his sarcophagus, was grating and thunderous.

Scipio stood, the earth shaking under his feet, as the dreadnought charged a greenskin war machine. The sergeant marvelled as Agnathio tore the last diminutive ork dreadnought apart. Crushing its can-like body with a blow from its massive power fist, Agnathio then wrenched the weapon free before thrusting it back into the cavity he'd created and churned the ork pilot within to bloody mulch.

'*For the Chapter, forward!*' roared the implacable dreadnought, breaking apart a huddle of gretchin clutching crudely-made bombs with his power fist's built-in storm bolter.

'Thunderbolts regroup,' Scipio barked, recovering his chainsword from where it had jammed in the ork dreadnought's cannon. Bereft of his battle helm's comm-feed, he had to shout.

Mercifully, they were still at full strength. Garrik and Brakkius had recovered; Largo and Ortus, chewed up by the dreadnought's cannon, were also battle-ready, albeit with punctured power armour. Only Hekor staggered, the jagged chest wound having clotted thanks to the Larraman cells in his blood. The organ that generated them was a crucial part of a Space Marine's genetically-enhanced physiology. Without it, Hekor would be dead.

'Still with us, brother?' asked Scipio.

'On your lead, Sergeant Vorolanus,' Hekor replied, biting back the pain, and cradling his flamer against his ruined chest.

Scipio nodded.

'To the Chaplain,' he ordered. 'Form up on Brother Agnathio.'

The dense *crump* of the garrison's artillery was deafening, and sent violent tremors rippling through the earth with every discharge. Scipio's Lyman's Ear filtered out the noise, regulated it to tolerable levels, and maintained his balance with every resulting shell quake.

The north wall of Ghospora Hive was only a hundred metres away.

Once Agnathio had finished off the mob of greenskin dreadnoughts, the tactical squads had linked up with Chaplain Orad quickly. Like Scipio, Iulus and Praxor had escaped without sustaining any fatalities, though they were battered and war-weary.

Using the vox-unit in his gorget like a loud hailer, Chaplain Orad bellowed battle-prayers to lift the spirits of the Ultramarines and galvanise them. They would need to be girded – with the black walls of Ghospora at hand, the teeth of the greenskin elites were next.

The fighting was harder this close to the hive defences. The orks here were a different breed: bigger, with heavier armour; some encased in entirely mechanical suits replete with power claws and mounted heavy weapons. Their skin was darker, almost black, thick and ornery like flak armour. This was Zanzag's mob, his inner circle, his clan.

'For Marneus Calgar and the Chapter!' roared Chaplain Orad, and Scipio echoed his cry as the Thunderbolts charged.

Hordes of lesser greenskins surrounded the core of Zanzag's elite; the Ultramarines tore through them with bolter and blade. Scipio fought one of the scar-faced ork veterans. The beast was huge, clad in thick plate, its muscled arms augmented by a crude array of pneumatic pistons to enhance its strength. A plume of flame spilled out of the ork's arm attachment, which was fended off by Scipio's vambrace before he got close and hacked it off with his chainsword. It waded in with a snapping power claw that the Ultramarine barely dodged. Bolt pistol rounds exploded against its torso, but the smoking armour showed only dents and chipped paint. A second veteran loomed alongside it, and Scipio suddenly felt outmatched.

A fierce storm of promethium sent it reeling as Brother Hekor came up in support. But the greenskin endured, wading through the intense conflagration before letting rip with some kind of custom cannon mounted on one arm. Fat shells spat from the muzzle like metal rain, and Hekor was torn apart. The ork grunted in what could only have been cruel mirth.

The Ultramarine's power armour was wrecked; it hadn't even slowed the bullets.

Scipio took an involuntary step back, hacking at a lesser greenskin that got too close. Three of his squad fired in unison at Hekor's cackling slayer. The sergeant added his own weapon to the fusillade, and the ork finally went down. The second stomped in, looking for a kill, when Chaplain Orad intervened and crushed the beast's skull with a blow from his crozius.

'Do not falter,' he roared, plasma pistol blazing. 'We must reach Captain Sicarius. Let nothing prevent it. In the name of Guilliman, advance!' A furious barrage of ork fire spattered against his rosarius field. Rounds exploded in front of his skull-faced visage, Orad didn't even flinch. He forged in again, bellowing litanies of retribution and cleansing. Scipio and the rest of the Ultramarines followed him further into the horde. The sergeant could discern the hulking forms of the Terminators of Squad Helios ahead through the chaos.

The battle was a deadly grind now, but Zanzag's officer cadre was as intractable as the bulwarks that they fought to bring down. Every metre gained was a blood-baptised struggle. The custom weapons fashioned by some inexplicable freak of greenskin science were proving effective, and taking a toll. Power armour, it seemed, was no proof against them. In the last few minutes alone, Scipio had seen three battle-brothers fall to the ork veterans wielding them.

The Ultramarines adapted, concentrating fire on these greenskins to take them down, using the heavy weapons advancing from the rearguard devastator squads to tear up the ork armour. Brother Agnathio leant his multi-melta to the barrage, the super-heated beam scything through the enemy, before crashing forward through the mass to stave in a veteran's skull with his power fist.

Up ahead, Scipio saw a gaping crevice in Ghospora's bastion wall where the greenskins had breached it. Scores of dead Sable Gunners, Black Reach's human garrison, littered the rubble around it. Corpses piled high like macabre sandbags as the valiant but hopeless defenders pressed more men into the gap in a desperate effort to staunch it. Through the blood-soaked melee, Scipio caught sight of an even larger beast, its armour and trappings more impressive and ostentatious than the other greenskins. It too wielded a customised cannon and clutched a hefty axe, crackling with electrical energy, in its other mighty fist. A wall of densely armoured ork warriors surrounded it, even more scarred and leathery than the rest. A bodyguard.

Zanzag. It could be no other.

The snatched glimpse was fleeting, lost in the pitch and yaw of the firefight. Scipio dug in, hewing with his chainsword as it growled for blood. His warriors were around him, fighting hard; Chaplain Orad too, hurling vitriolic rhetoric at the orks. If they didn't understand his words, they felt the bite of his fury with every stroke of his crozius.

In a wash of blood and screaming death they had broken through. Scipio found himself alongside the massive Terminators of 1st Company as they released an explosive tempest with their storm bolters. Through the carnage, the battle din throbbing in his ears, the scent of sweat and flame filling his nostrils, Scipio thought he saw Arcus Helios forging a body-strewn path with his thunder hammer.

Then he saw Sicarius. The captain was at the vanguard of the attack, his Lions guarding his flank and rear as he pressed ahead of the main battle group, slaying orks with every blow. Faced with a mob of three greenskin scar-veterans, Sicarius dispatched them with impudent sweeps of his ancient power sword. The brutal act of bravura created a few metres of ground for the Ultramarines to exploit, allowing them to contest the breach itself.

Sicarius stormed into it without thought. Squad Solinus was at his heels, just like at Fort Telendrar.

The captain's iron-hard gaze was fixed ahead, Scipio catching snatched glimpses of him through the spraying blood and muzzle flashes as he fought to keep pace. The sergeant powered into the breach alongside Chaplain Orad, Squad Helios and his other battle-brothers, determined to cleanse it of greenskins and liberate the hive. The captain, though, had but one enemy in mind. He wanted Zanzag, and he meant to get him regardless of the foes arrayed in his path.

'Brothers!' Sicarius roared, strafing a white-hot beam of plasma from his pistol into the greenskin ranks. 'War calls. Will you answer?' He thrust the Tempest Blade into the air like a beacon, the 2nd Company banner, held aloft by Brother Vandius, snapping as its backdrop.

The Ultramarines roared in unison, Scipio amongst them, redoubling their efforts. Fusillades of bolter fire and swathes of promethium pounded into the breach. Churning blades and crackling power weapons followed in the bloody aftermath as the Astartes closed again.

With Sicarius leading them, the Ultramarines were an unstoppable force.

Victory was near. Scipio could feel the spine of the ork horde slowly breaking as the punishment inflicted by the Ultramarines began to take its toll.

They just had to press a little harder.

Rushing into a gap made by the awesome firepower of the dreadnoughts that were consolidating the Ultramarines' position, Scipio came within scant metres of the heroic captain. Scipio found his own prowess enhanced, his will like iron in the reflected glory of his leader. He saw Iulus and Praxor close by, similarly affected.

Chaplain Orad was intent on meting out death, smiting the orks with shots from his plasma pistol and arcing blows from his crozius.

Brother Agnathio, overtaken in the charge, was laying waste to the remaining greenskin armour from the rear of the Ultramarines' spearhead contesting the breach. Brother Ultracius fought alongside him, unleashing hell from his assault cannon; two goliaths venting storm and fury.

Through sheer aggression and the rate of attrition being suffered by the foe at their vengeful hand, the Ultramarines forced the greenskins out of the Ghospora bastion defences. The Sable Gunners swarmed over recently liberated positions, taking up heavy weapon emplacements, pouring las-fire into the horde from behind ruined walls and shattered watch towers.

Scipio admired their bravery. Humans were brittle, weak even, compared to an Astartes. Their minds and mores were crude and undeveloped, but they had spirit.

The tide turning, and with the walls of Ghospora at their backs, Scipio and his other battle-brothers dug in for the final battle. Cutting his own name into the pages of glory with his chainsword, Scipio noticed Captain Sicarius finally catch sight of his prey. The ork warlord, Zanzag, had retreated from the breach further down the wall and was bellowing loudly at his troops in a rage, thick wads of sputum flicking

from his maw. The beast was throwing everything
he had at the Ultramarines, trying to retake the
wall by hurling waves after wave of orks into the
meatgrinder.

Zanzag's death would end it all. No greenskin was
as tenacious without its leader.

Sicarius sighted down his pistol, but the weapon
was smacked from his grasp before he could fire by
another scar-veteran. The captain gutted it with his
power sword, and cried, 'Daceus!'

The veteran sergeant of his Lions reacted instinc-
tively and threw his bolter to the captain who caught
it smoothly and fired one-handed. He roared as the
muzzle-flash lit his face; Scipio thought he had never
seen a visage so terrifying.

The explosive rounds rippled through the air, arrest-
ing Zanzag's frothing tirade as his maw and most of
his trunk-like neck were hit. Scipio saw blood spurt,
and thick chips of tusk fly, but the beast did not
fall. Instead, he retreated, allowing the remnants of
his bodyguard to protect him. The other greenskins
pressed, too, bullied into becoming flesh-shields for
their warlord's escape.

The fight, it seemed, had gone out of them. The
orks were in full retreat.

Cheers erupted from the Sable Gunners in exultation of their saviours. The scattered cries of the
defenders echoed around empty towers, eclipsing
the plaintive moaning of the wounded. The garrison was down to bare bones after the beating they'd
been given, but they could still muster some heart
in the face of unexpected triumph.

'Victoris Ultra!' bellowed Chaplain Orad, lifting his crozius high.

The resultant response from the Ultramarines was a roar that resounded across the battlefield.

Ghospora was won.

PHASE THREE – ORK HUNTERS

'Well met, Iulus,' called Scipio, seeing his fellow sergeant approaching through the ruins of the Ghospora bastion wall.

It was barely half an hour after the orks had been defeated, and engineers had already set about repairing the cavernous breach made by the greenskins. Demolition crews scurried in packs, trailing spools of wire as they fled behind the still-standing wall sections and pressed down the plungers of their crude equipment to set off explosives. A crushed tower collapsed a few metres away from Iulus, crashing down into the breach and partially filling it in.

The shaven-headed sergeant ignored it, ploughing through the dust cloud to reach Scipio on the other side.

'Glad to see you're still alive, brother.' Scipio clasped

Iulus's hand in a firm grasp, and his fellow Ultramarine clapped his arm in return.

'Aye,' growled Iulus, wiping a bead of sweat from his shiny forehead, 'though it looks like I should be saying that to you.' He pointed a gauntleted finger towards the other sergeant's forehead.

Scipio touched it and felt a gash from a wound he hadn't realised he'd sustained. He remembered the close call against the ork dreadnought.

'Just a flesh wound,' he replied.

'Seven dead,' remarked Iulus tersely, gazing out at the killing field beyond Ghospora's north wall where a host of corpses lay, predominantly ork. Scipio saw Apothecary Venatio moving amongst the death-smog, poised with his reductor to extract the gene-seed from the fallen so that they might fight again, albeit in a new body with a different mind, their legacy preserved and serving the Chapter even in death.

A Space Marine combat squad accompanied him, retrieving the bodies of their dead battle-brothers so they could be laid to rest with honour and their equipment salvaged for re-use by the company.

'Fifteen wounded,' Iulus concluded, as he looked away.

'It's grim work,' agreed Scipio. 'Hekor was amongst the fallen,' he added darkly.

'He will serve the Chapter in death, just as we all will,' offered Iulus, somewhat pragmatically.

'At least victory is ours,' said Scipio, watching as Chaplain Orad moved through the carnage too, sporadic bursts erupting from his plasma pistol as he executed any greenskins that still clung tenaciously to life. He was also there to provide last rites for any fallen Astartes that could not be saved. Apothecary and Chaplain worked in tandem. Orad knelt by the stricken body of one of Scipio's battle-brothers, giving a final benediction before Venatio moved in.

The dreadnoughts Ultracius and Agnathio roved in the distance like terrible avengers, patrolling the dormant warzone for lingering greenskin forces, adding to the already considerable death toll.

'Victory? I take it you have not heard.'

'Heard what?' asked Scipio, nonplussed, his attention back on Iulus.

'The captain's quarry eluded him. We press for the wastelands beyond the hive city, where the orks have made their transient camp.'

'Brothers!' The voice of Praxor forestalled Scipio's response. The sergeant was jubilant as he made his way through the bustling humans and the Chapter's Techmarines with their gaggles of mindless servitors. Every effort was being made to secure Ghospora Hive before the Ultramarines moved on.

'The glory of the Chapter has swelled this day,' he said, nodding proudly. 'To fight at Sicarius's side…' he added, shaking his head in awe at the memory of it. 'Did you feel his aura, Scipio? Never have I been so lifted. Never has pistol and blade felt as righteous.'

'It was indeed humbling,' Scipio said, bowing his head in reverence. The sight of Sicarius surging through the horde was the substance of legend, and here he had witnessed it first hand.

'Heroic, I'll concede that,' countered Iulus, his slab-like face turning to granite, 'but reckless. My

squad was lucky to have reached the battlefront at
all, as I dare say others were. To lead is one thing,
to leave your charges behind in the pursuit of personal glory is quite another.'

Praxor's voice hardened. Scipio thought he heard
his fists clench.

'Still fighting Agemman's corner, I see.' The glaring
sergeant's tone was even.

'I fight no corner, save that of the Chapter.' Iulus
turned, and was about to walk away when the voice
of Veteran Sergeant Daceus stopped him.

'Sergeants,' he growled, to none of them in particular. 'The captain requests your presence in the
prima-factorum.'

The Ultramarines, so divided by opinion, saluted
as one and followed the Lion of Macragge as he led
them away.

Ghospora Hive was a vast edifice of sprawling industry. Much of that industry was now in ruins, but still
the fact and the echo of it remained. Towers surged
into the darkness of myriad levels above. Walkways
and gantries criss-crossed each other like some infer-
nal metallic lattice. Habitation blocks and worker
tenements clustered together in ranks like bedraggled
parade troopers huddling against the rough elements.
Immense hexagonal stacks from the mineral-mining
complexes bored into the sublevels vented smoke and
gas in thick plumes. Cranes arched over open-topped
ore silos like broken fingers. Immense gears, looping
cables and lengths of track – constituent parts of the
gargantuan mining engine that enabled Black Reach

to function, export, trade and to live – pervaded over all. So vast, its population once numbering billions, the hive city was now reduced to a broken remnant of what it had once been.

The area immediately beyond the wall had been heavily industrialised and comprised several shattered factorum buildings – boxy structures with a plain, austere appearance.

'Functional' was the word that entered Scipio's mind as they followed Veteran Sergeant Daceus into the only building that had avoided being shelled by the greenskins and was more or less still standing.

Sodium lighting bolted up in strips across a ferrocrete ceiling cast little luminescence into a hexagonal chamber. Debris and scattered refuse had been swept into the edges of the room, and a large metal conference table with assorted chairs and stools stood in the centre. There were several antechambers, some cordoned off by rough sheets of plastek, others drenched in gloom. Soot coated everything, and drifted from the ceiling in fitful motes turning the light grainy. Brownish stains ran down the wall in one of the corners from a ruptured water pipe that had been bandaged by an old bullet-ridden flak jacket. It was a poor fix, and the sodden piece of Imperial Guard-issue equipment dripped languidly into a murky pool below.

Scipio noted all of this in the first few seconds as he entered the chamber. All in all it was a rat-infested pit, barely fit for serfs.

'My lords–' A human had approached the Ultramarines as soon as they had arrived, and prostrated himself on the ground before them. 'You have saved us all this glorious day.' The man wore the black uniform and silver cuirass of a Sable Gunners officer. 'I am Corporal Vormast, commander of the 81st, 23rd and 15th Sable Gunner regiments. Welcome to Ghospora Operational Headquarters.'

Struggling to his feet, a clearly awe-struck aide assisting him, Corporal Vormast was a wretched specimen. His armour was tarnished, his uniform dirty and torn. The troopers he had in his charge behind him were raw and ragged, many swathed in bandage and gauze.

Scipio regarded the men with pity. They had given their all and still would have been bested by the greenskins had it not been for the Space Marines' intervention. Iulus showed only cold indifference; to him the corporal was no different to the rock of the walls or the metal of the hive's guns – they were all just materiel. Praxor's expression was one of utter disdain. He looked above the man, or rather maintained Astartes eye-level, searching for the presence of his captain, but none was to be found.

'Captain Sicarius will be with us shortly,' said Daceus, as if guessing Praxor's thoughts, walking past the human and his retinue. 'Corporal Vormast, please join us at the command table,' he added without looking back.

The human gave up his genuflecting, his deference on hiatus, and scurried over to the giant Astartes who had left him in their wake.

'A corporal,' Scipio remarked when the human

officer had caught them up. 'That is a low rank for one in charge of the defence of an entire hive city.'

'Yes,' Vormast replied a little nervously. Scipio thought he looked young for such a post. 'I am the highest-ranking officer left,' the human told them, removing his corporal's cap and wiping a sweat-drenched mop of hair beneath before replacing it. 'The greenskins hit us hard.'

'I'll say,' Praxor muttered under his breath, casting a contemptuous look around the festering sinkhole that was Sable Gunner Command.

A large blast door opened, spilling in grey light and the raucous sounds of engineers striving to repair the wall defences.

Captain Sicarius strode through the opening. He had his battle helm clasped beneath his arm and his voluminous cloak billowed as he walked. The Tempest Blade was cleaned and sheathed at his hip. Even for the other Astartes, he was a stirring sight. Only Iulus appeared unmoved.

Two other warriors, almost as impressive, accompanied him: one, the towering form of Arcus Helios stomping loudly in his Terminator armour, the other was Brother-Sergeant Telion, slighter but no less dangerous and imposing.

'Brothers,' said Sicarius upon reaching the table, regarding each of the Ultramarines in turn before setting his helmet upon the metal surface. He then lowered his gaze, glowering slightly at Corporal Vormast, aloof and in many ways as alien to the diminutive human as the ork was to him.

'Rest easy, commander,' he said, putting a giant

armoured hand on the corporal's shoulder. The man tried to muster some presence despite his tarnished silver carapace and ripped brocade, but he only came up to the edge of the Space Marine's plastron. Sicarius looked down on him like a man regarding an infant.

'The north wall is secure, the greenskin are broken,' he continued. 'Tell me now, where in the wastelands does the warlord make his lair? Answer quickly,' he warned, 'my gunships are already on their way here.'

Following Zanzag's escape, Sicarius had immediately ordered three additional gunships – *Pilium, Spatha* and *Xiphos* – sent from the *Valin's Revenge* to convey those elements of the battle group that had not entered the battle via drop pod assault. To the captain's mind, time was now at a premium. He wanted the ork dead, by his hand, and the deed done with the utmost haste. The High Suzerain's glory, it seemed, would not wait.

Vormast bowed curtly at the Space Marine captain's command, seemingly unable to speak for the moment, and shuffled around the edge of the command table to a small panel fused to one side. After pressing a sequence of icons, an expanse of platen glass flickered to life on the table's surface, backlit by sodium bulbs.

Scipio saw Praxor sneer at the crude technology. Iulus, too, appeared unimpressed, likely wondering how Ghospora hadn't already fallen before the Emperor's Angels had arrived on streams of fire from the sky.

As the image behind the platen glass resolved, a

map of Ghospora Hive and the surrounding area appeared – Sable, the northern continent. The view was top-down, the landscape expressed in gradients, contour lines and hues of mineral density. Principally it was a mining chart co-opted for use as a campaign map. Three hive cities stood out, marked Lylith, Sulphora and, of course, Ghospora itself.

'Lylith is destroyed,' muttered Vormast, partially to himself as if in bitter confirmation of the fact, scouring the map quickly.

Scipio absorbed the details in an instant, committing them to eidetic memory.

Ghospora's nearest neighbour was Sulphora Hive to the south, a few hundred kilometres distant. The wasteland that lay between them was riddled with artificial valleys, dredging gullies and mountainous sandbanks, all interwoven by a web of black tributaries – Black Reach's polluted, carbon-rich rivers. Many crossed and weaved like livid veins; others sprawled and stretched in thick, dark belts.

The largest and widest of the rivers flowed between both of the hives, and was named Blackwallow on the map. One of its minor tributaries fed into a narrow ravine, ringed by a dense forest, called Black Gulch. The mighty river then drove east until it fell off a sheer cliff in a waterfall. An expanse of water to the north-east, several thousand kilometres from Ghospora, and fringing the northern continent, was marked the Sable Sea.

Scipio assumed this was the reason the orks had not sacked the hive city sooner. It would have taken time to cross. The Imperial defenders would likely have erected blockades, mined the deep waters and sent vessels to impede the attackers. He imagined fleets of burning ships adrift on an oily sea, gutted and forlorn. A hopeless sacrifice against a brutal and implacable invader.

'The greenskins took Cobalt, Kohl and Stygia with almost no warning,' the corporal explained, surveying the map with a dull gaze. He scrolled the northern continent east, using a dial – Scipio noticed the human's hand shaking; doubtless from shellshock or some other nervous condition he'd developed over the course of Ghospora's defence – and the other neighbouring continents were revealed on a previously hidden area of the map. Each had three hive cities. All, barring those on Sable, had been sacked by the orks.

'Two months, nine hives,' said Iulus, partly to himself, partly to his battle-brothers. 'The orks must have struck quickly and precisely. It's not a tactic they're known for.'

'Any thoughts on how that could be possible, Sergeant Fennion?' asked Sicarius, directly.

Iulus kept looking at the map, as if the answer to the captain's question could be discerned there. His demeanour was iron-hard as ever, even beneath the High Suzerain's scrutiny.

'A water-borne ship of some kind,' he said. 'They'd need a fleet to cross the sea. It would have to be a vessel large enough to ferry an entire horde. It's the only way the orks could have marshalled an assault so swiftly, possibly even coordinated multiple strikes.'

'You believe the greenskin capable of such cohesion.'

The bone-hard voice of Telion seemed to chill the room as he spoke. It wasn't a challenge, just a statement of fact.

Even Iulus paused as the intimidating scout sergeant stepped into the light-glare thrown from the platen glass.

The slab-faced Sergeant Iulus met Telion's icy gaze in spite of the veteran's formidable presence. 'I don't know what they're capable of, brother-sergeant. They're alien. Who can truly say what goes on in their depraved minds, what thought processes drive and impel them.'

'So it is possible, then?'

'Yes, it is possible,' Iulus replied at length.

Telion nodded, as if satisfied, and Scipio felt the tension bleed back out of the room and some of the warmth return.

'Your watch towers and sentries,' said Iulus, 'did they detect any vessels capable of delivering an assault of this nature?'

'No, my lord,' replied Corporal Vormast, 'they did not. Once they'd crossed the Sable Sea, we saw no more ships. The greenskins just emerged from the water banks, swarming towards us in their thousands. Vox-casts from Colonel Nachthausser at Arachnis and then Captain Oben at Eusthenos indicated the same pattern before we lost contact...' The corporal's voice trailed off, and Scipio imagined the desperate pleas for aid, the gunfire and screaming in the background until static swallowed all sounds of life, and the irrefutable truth that Vormast's superiors were dead seeped its way insidiously into his marrow.

Iulus fell silent, unaware of the corporal's grief, instead seeing threads of strategy in his mind's eye and trying to unravel them to get at the truth of the orks' lightning raids.

'We would have seen their ships,' the man said at last. 'There's no way they could have concealed them.'

'Something else then,' suggested Scipio. 'Some bastardised machinery of ork science we have yet to encounter?'

'Our Techmarines recovered some of the weapons the greenskins used to pierce our slain brothers' power armour with such ease,' Veteran Sergeant Daceus remarked. 'It suggests this Zanzag is no ordinary beast.'

'It has some mechanical acumen, it would seem,' Praxor put in, not wishing to be left out of the strategic analysis. 'Do we know how these crude technologies fare against tactical dreadnought armour?'

Arcus Helios spoke for the first time since entering the chamber. He had removed his Terminator helmet. His head, complete with its shaven crest of white hair bifurcating his otherwise smooth skull, looked absurdly small encased within the massive armoured suit and almost touched the sodium strip lighting.

'We engaged the greenskin scar-veterans,' he said, his stentorian voice echoing loudly. His sheer presence and enormous size made the humans balk. 'Our armour proved impervious. The crux terminatus left us unscathed.'

'The very fact that the warlord eluded our wrath shows it is a singular beast,' Praxor remarked.

'It shows its fortune, its strong survival instinct – that is all,' said Sicarius.

Scipio thought the captain's clipped and even tone suggested another emotion: his profound dissatisfaction at allowing the creature to escape him. '*My spike*' – he recalled Sicarius's words spoken on the *Valin's Revenge*.

'And luck will always run out, Sergeant Manorian.'

'Yes sir.' Praxor rasped the words a little, clearing his throat afterwards as surreptitiously as he could.

'So then, corporal–' Sicarius concluded, returning his gaze to the slightly cowering human and his retinue. 'My quarry?'

'Your scouts–' said Vormast, mustering his voice again. 'Your scouts' reports match our own intelligence. The few long-range antenna feeds that remain operational monitored the greenskin horde retreating to here,' – the corporal pointed to the wasteland between Ghospora and its other intact neighbour, Sulphora – 'where the orks have constructed a series of fortresses from the salvage taken from the sacked hives.'

Sicarius's face hardened. Scipio thought he saw a brief glint in his eye at the thought of catching up to Zanzag and exacting his revenge for the ork having eluded him the first time.

The dense pitch of Thunderhawk turbofans decelerating to landing speed resonated loudly through the cracks in the prima-factorum building and curtailed further analysis. The transports had arrived right on time.

'Gather your squads,' Sicarius muttered darkly,

sweeping up his helmet, 'we deploy for the waste-land at once. Full attack. We'll teach this alien scum what it means to incur the ire of the Ultramarines.'

'My lord–' The Astartes were already walking away when Corporal Vormast spoke up. 'My own troops are severely reduced in strength, our walls are in tat-ters,' he implored. 'Should the orks return, we will be defenceless.'

'No servant of the Emperor is ever defenceless, cor-poral,' Sicarius told him, deigning to turn and face the man before jamming on his helmet. 'Faith pro-tects us all.'

'Of course, my liege,' the corporal persisted, licking his lips nervously, 'but–'

'But you'll feel better with the might of the Asta-rtes at your back,' Sicarius interjected, his voice tinny and resonant through his helmet vox. 'Provision has already been made to galvanise Ghospora, corpo-ral. The Ultramarines will guarantee your protection.

'Brother-Sergeant Telion,' the captain added, turn-ing to the master scout before departing with the other Space Marines.

The blast doors were opening already. Scipio saw Sergeant Solinus waiting there with news of the Thunderhawks' arrival.

'Brother-Sergeants Manorian and Fennion.' Teli-on's voice stopped both Astartes in their tracks. 'The Shield Bearers and the Immortals with Squad Tirian will man the garrison in case the orks return,' he said without further explanation, before following Sicarius.

Scipio watched Praxor fall into step behind them

as he left Sable Gunner Operational Command. The sergeant of the Shield Bearers was crestfallen, his desire to find glory and honour at his captain's side punctured. It couldn't have been any worse had Sicarius taken a dagger and plunged it through his heart. Iulus, on the other hand, seemed utterly unmoved. He would simply do his duty, as he always did.

In seconds the room was empty again, except for Corporal Vormast and his men. He pored over the campaign map, visualising the fallen battlelines, the broken fortifications and the droves of dead troopers sacrificed to stem the ork tide. How many more would it take to rid them of the greenskin menace, he wondered?

'You didn't think he would leave you behind, did you, Praxor?' asked Iulus. He was looking through a pair of magnoculars and scouring the sand storms kicked up in the wake of the Ultramarines' battle group leaving Ghospora. Together with his enhanced Astartes eye-sight and the magnification offered by the device, Iulus could see many kilometres with crystal clarity. The Thunderhawks moved in squadron formation, kicking up plumes of dust as they flew low over the sandy plains. The quartet of deadly gunships conveyed the bulk of the squads, whilst alongside a pair of Storm-variant land speeders soared ahead, carrying Telion and his scouts on advanced reconnaissance.

Gladius led the wing of Thunderhawks. Like its commander, it seemed eager to close with the orks. Somewhere amongst them, though, rode Scipio.

'Fight well,' muttered Iulus, 'and don't get yourself killed.'

'Captain Sicarius has entrusted us with this Imperial bastion,' Praxor replied to Iulus's earlier remark. 'We should be honoured to receive such a charge.'

Praxor did not sound as if he were honoured; his tone smacked heavily of disappointment.

Iulus lowered the magnoculars, passing them to a Sable Gunner sergeant close by. The two Space Marines were standing on the uppermost ramparts of the Ghospora bastion wall right above where the human engineers, under the guidance of the Techmarines, had patched the breach. Iulus was greatly experienced at siege defence, having trained under Captain Lysander himself. It was for this reason he had been left to organise the Ghosporan defence, though, as his superior, Praxor was still technically in charge. Deeming the breach as the point of greatest vulnerability, Iulus had concentrated the Astartes forces there.

Above them, stationed in an armour-reinforced watchtower, stood Sergeant Tirian and his devastator squad. The lofty vantage point offered an unparalleled view of the open ground beyond, a killing field for his heavy weapons.

'You are a bad liar, brother.' Iulus's glare was penetrating as he turned it on Praxor.

'What glory is there in minding the humans,' he said at last, in a tone that only Iulus could hear.

'Sicarius is concerned for his glory alone,' the stone-faced sergeant replied. 'His rash and unconsidered deployment to the wastelands is an indicator of that.' Iulus's attention was abruptly commanded elsewhere. His eyes narrowed as he looked back out across the sand flats.

'I wouldn't worry about your own laurels, Brother Praxor,' he said after a short pause. A grin split his features as he turned to the other Ultramarine. Like all Space Marines, he was a warrior forged, and exulted in battle. 'The orks are coming.' Iulus pointed northwards, towards a glittering black horizon.

Praxor followed the line of the sergeant's gauntleted finger and saw the smoke clouds of a massive horde of orks heading their way.

'The warlord split his forces,' he muttered.

'Drawing off the bulk of our battle-brothers, thus emboldening his larger reserves to renew the Ghospora assault,' Iulus concluded, making for the wrought-iron staircase that led to ground level.

'Courage and honour, brother,' he said, patting Praxor on the pauldron as he passed him.

'Courage and honour,' Praxor replied, a belligerent cast affecting his face as he followed.

The Ultramarines sergeants descended to the wall breach where eighteen of their battle-brothers awaited them, split into four combat squads. Soon they would be deployed along the wall, ready to repel the ork invaders.

Techmarine Lascar was also present, a final concession from Captain Sicarius to secure the hive city. The heavily augmented student of the Adeptus Mechanicus approached Iulus as soon as he had alighted from the stairs.

'Blessings of the Omnissiah, Brother Fennion,'

intoned Lascar, invoking the benediction of the Martian tech-aspect of the Emperor as if by mechanistic rote.

Iulus had always thought there was an autonomous quality about the Techmarine's voice, as if whatever scant emotions he'd possessed prior to his long years of training on Mars to be inducted into the ranks of the Mechanicus had left him almost a machine himself. Sergeant Fennion was ignorant of the clandestine rituals of the Martian adepts but their influence upon his battle-brother was plain to see.

Lascar was clad in the MkVII battle plate of his fellow Ultramarines, but wore the cog icon of the Adeptus Mechanicus on the lower portion of his plastron. The stark device indicated his fealty to the Martian creed. An immense servo-harness was affixed to Lascar's back, hard-wired into the hefty generator for his power armour. It consisted of several pneumatic servo-arms, a lifter array, flamer attachment and various esoteric tools attached to the ends of snaking mechadendrites, including a las-torch, plasma-cutter and vibro-saw.

Two bent-backed servitors accompanied him. The partially lobotomised automatons were armour-clad and heaved slow and clicking breaths through metal respirator masks. Mono-tasked as combat models, each servitor carried a weapon mount affixed to its torso in place of an amputated arm. A belt-fed heavy bolter whirred up and down with concealed motorisation on one; a bulky plasma gun linked up to a massive generator hummed dully on the other.

The adepts of the Red Planet, worshippers of the

Machine God who craved metal over flesh in their pursuit of oneness with the Omnissiah, had schooled Lascar, as they had schooled all of Astartes Techmarines, in the ways of the machine-spirit and the art of repairing vehicles and weapons. Lascar's knowledge in this regard was without peer amongst the small battle group and Iulus knew the Techmarine's expertise might well be the difference between victory and death when the greenskins reached the walls.

'All is in readiness,' Lascar announced, mechadendrites twitching, reflecting his own ardency to smite the greenskins.

'And your tactical assessment of the Ghosporan natives?' asked Iulus, careful to avoid looking at the servitors directly. The melding of necrotic flesh and metal felt somehow distasteful, despite his own genetically-engineered apotheosis.

'The garrison is at forty-three per cent effective strength.'

'Not much,' remarked Praxor, his opinion how little the humans were worth obvious.

'It will have to be enough,' growled Iulus, cranking a round into the breach of his bolt pistol. 'What of our ordnance?'

'The Thunderfire cannons have been blessed and the Rites of Accuracy and Functioning performed,' Lascar replied.

Behind him, Iulus could see the first of the Space Marine support guns grinding into position at empty cannon emplacements on thick, armoured tracks. Unlike most other Astartes artillery, the Thunderfire cannon was designed with static defence in mind.

The broad, quad-barrelled guns were pintle-mounted and capable of unleashing a devastating barrage of surface, air or subterranean-adaptive shells. Within the packed ranks of the greenskins they would reap bloody havoc.

Iulus smiled grimly at the sight of the massive cannon.

'Let the earth tremble,' he said.

Scipio stared blankly out of the occuliport of the *Xiphos*. The dark sand banks of Black Reach flicked by in a slowly increasing blur as the gunship picked up speed and increased loft. The ruins of a ramshackle ork fortress lay burning in the Thunderhawk's wake. Scipio could see the smoke coiling from its wreckage even when they soared to three hundred metres. It had been little more than a shanty town, a brutish amalgam of vehicle husks, wrought-iron plating and crude barricades, a rally point of sorts. Sicarius had sacked three such encampments on the edge of the Blackwallow already, purged them with cleansing fire and salvos from the Thunderhawks' heavy bolters. Naught but churned earth, blood and greenskin pyres rewarded him. Zanzag had not been amongst the dead.

The Thunderhawk gunship was a singular vessel. Three powerful motors fuelled by an on-board fusion reactor provided speed and manoeuvrability that would rival most conventional Imperial fighters, and without the need to compromise firepower. This, the gunship had in abundance. Four remote turrets of twin-linked heavy bolters patrolled the front fuselage and wings, slaved to the Space Marine gunner's control panel on the flight deck. A twin-linked lascannon protruded from the prow like a lance to tackle heavy armour. Finally, an immense dorsal-mounted turbo-laser on a fixed turret provided serious destructive potential, backed up by a payload of six Hellstrike missiles.

Despite the generous amount of munitions and the need to maximise the vessel's Astartes transport capacity, there was still room enough for a small reclusiam, a two-person shrine annexed from the upper transport hold where warriors could pray and take their oaths.

It was within the cool sanctity of the *Xiphos's* reclusiam that Scipio found himself kneeling, head bowed with his eyes closed. Having seen enough through the occuliport, Scipio had left his battle-brothers, together with the warriors of Squad Octavian and the mighty Agnathio, rattling in his transit scaffold, in the Chamber Sanctuarine. It was the principle transport hold of the ship, where the Astartes would wait in their alcoves for the order to deploy.

'A pure and pious mind is one that serves the Emperor,' a voice like shifting ashes issued from the shadows in the reclusiam.

Scipio was laying down his bolter reverently when he looked up, incredulous that he had not noticed the other figure in the small chamber.

'Your devotion is to be lauded, Brother Vorolanus,' rasped Chaplain Orad, leaning forward slightly as if to officially announce his presence.

Scipio tried not to react as he regarded him. The

Chaplain went unhooded. His skull helm was set alongside him as he knelt. The sergeant of the Thunderbolts saw the suggestion of the horrific scarring that marred his visage. Pink tissue flared angrily in the wan light of votive candles. The flesh was twisted, and one half of the Chaplain's lip was burned away revealing bone and teeth. His left ear was ruined, barely a void in the side of his head, all form and shape to it eaten away by bio-acid. And the eye... the eye stared always, its cornea bloodshot and glowering, the lid long since eroded. Scipio wondered if Orad could still see out of it.

'I watched you as you entered, brother,' he told Scipio, his blighted eye seeming to swell with a sudden change in mood. 'Something troubles you, yes?'

Scipio considered a lie, but dismissed the notion immediately; it would be dishonourable. Furthermore, Chaplain Orad would discover the deceit before it left Scipio's lips. It was as if that red-eyed gaze could penetrate the very depths of his soul. Instead, Scipio chose to remain silent.

'Would you like to recite a liturgy with me or perhaps one of the Canticles of Hera, the Cassius Catechism mayhap?'

'You honour me, Brother-Chaplain, but it is not necessary.'

'You seek your answer in solitude, then?'

'I do, my brother.'

Orad stared a moment longer, that baleful red orb stripping away Scipio's defences like a laser, before he seemed satisfied and relented. The Chaplain donned his skull helm, much to Scipio's relief, and stood, muttering a benediction before the Imperial eagle symbol wrought into the facing wall.

'I am here for you, my son,' hissed Orad as he turned to leave. Through his helmet, his voice returned to its grating metallic timbre.

He gripped Scipio's pauldron as he spoke. The sergeant felt it like the weight of judgement on his shoulder. 'You have only to speak, and I will heed you.'

Once Orad had departed, his footfalls seemingly heavier and more resonant than his fellow Astartes, Scipio exhaled. He hadn't even realised he was holding his breath.

Confession would have to wait. In truth, there was little to confess, save that he felt the smallest kernel of doubt towards the actions of his captain. Since the sacking of the third ork fort, Scipio, in what few moments he had been in his presence, had witnessed a change in Sicarius. With each hour that the ork warlord continued to evade him, the captain was becoming more driven, more vehement, more... *reckless.*

Scipio railed at himself. Sicarius was a hero, the bravest of all of them, perhaps the finest Ultramarine in the entire Chapter. Why had Iulus's discontent plagued him so? Was the captain's eye really fixed on personal glory? Did he desire a place at the Chapter Master's right hand at the expense of Agemman? Arcus Helios was of 1st Company, and he seemed sanguine.

A presence at the chapel's entrance broke Scipio's introspection. He turned slowly, fearing for a moment that Chaplain Orad had returned to sermonise him after all. His mind eased when he saw Sergeant Octavian.

'My apologies for disturbing your orison, brother, but Captain Sicarius has convened a war council. We set down in twenty minutes.'

Scipio nodded his thanks, and Sergeant Octavian took it as his cue to return to the Chamber Sanctuarine. Donning his helmet, Scipio followed him, crushing the slivers of his doubts beneath the heel of his devotion to the Chapter.

The four Thunderhawks set down in a sandblasted clearing to the north-west of Black Gulch. The dark-veined ravine gushed below them through a thick crop of petrified trees. The gunships had landed in a square; ablative armour facing outwards, creating a ceramite-walled corral in which the Ultramarines could strategise their next move. In a planet overrun by orks, it was a prudent measure.

'Three greenskin forts in ruins,' Sicarius said to the assemblage of officers standing around the portable hololith map. A hazy rendition of the surrounding area in three-dimensional form issued from the spherical projector spiked into the ground. All of Sicarius's sergeants that had joined the battle group were present. Arcus Helios of 1st stood at the back like a giant sentinel, easily towering over his power-armoured battle-brothers. Scipio realised as he was standing amongst the officer cadre that he missed the presence of Iulus and Praxor. His fellow brothers were the closest thing to friends that he had in the Chapter. His bond with them both was very strong.

'Still we have no word, no sign of the beast – this *Zanzag*.' Sicarius scowled at the name, his noble countenance creasing with annoyance. 'This thorn must be excised,' he determined. 'I will draw it out and remove the poison that infects this planet. Nothing must stand in the way of this. Black Reach *will* be ours.'

'The northern continent is vast and the orks swarm over it. Two months is more than long enough to have erected several outposts, spread over hundreds of kilometres,' said Solinus, taking the opportunity to air his thoughts. 'We have sacked but three in a week. Our progress is too slow. The longer we delay, the longer the greenskins have to become further entrenched. We are righteous warriors of Calgar and the Emperor, but we are one hundred in a sea of thousands. What should be our next course of action?' Solinus asked of the group.

'A quadrant by quadrant search of this area,' offered Sergeant Helios, pointing over the shoulders of his battle-brothers to an area on the map that displayed Black Gulch and the location of the ork forts they had already destroyed. 'We go through the wastelands one grain at a time. Time consuming – yes, but what other recourse is there? Caverns, ravines, ruins: the greenskin must have made its lair somewhere. We have but to find it.'

Solinus nodded his approval reluctantly. A painstaking search appeared the only option. 'I will commence mapping out the search grid at once.'

'No,' Sicarius replied. The captain seemed distracted as he approached the hololith and began tracing his finger down one of the larger tributaries.

'Which river is this?'

'Blackwallow, my lord,' answered Scipio, as he tried to fathom his captain's thought processes. 'It has the widest and deepest of all the planet's river basins.'

'Lightning-fast assaults, coordinated and able to disappear without trace…' Sicarius regarded Scipio directly. The sergeant tried not to flinch before the face of the great hero. 'We followed but a half hour after the greenskins retreated from Ghospora, but found nothing of the warlord. How is that possible, brother-sergeant?'

'They are using the river,' Scipio decided. 'Something we haven't seen yet, something that eluded the watch stations of the Ghosporans themselves.'

'It fails to narrow down the search parameters,' observed Arcus Helios, deep voiced and commanding. 'We search by quadrants–'

'No…' Sicarius interjected calmly, his gaze on the hololith again. Scipio thought he saw a slight flicker of consternation cross the Terminator sergeant's face at the rebuttal. 'We are missing something,' Sicarius resumed. He almost muttered the words, as if he were speaking to himself. As if deciding there was nothing more to be gained from poring over the map image, Sicarius looked up. A moment later, a smile crept over his face as his mood changed.

'Our answer is coming.'

'My lord…' Sergeant Solinus began.

'We have but to wait,' Sicarius told them, looking over the sergeant's head at the distant horizon.

Scipio followed his gaze, along with the other sergeants. A land speeder hovered into view. On board were Telion and four of his scouts from the 10th.

The vehicle set down amidst the gathering, its baffled landing thrusters kicking up scuds of dust and propelling them into the hololith, making the device flicker and whirr noisily.

Veteran Sergeant Daceus knelt and switched it off to soothe its agitated machine spirit.

Telion leapt from the land speeder's open hatch before it had touched down, while its landing gear was still extending. He stalked over to Sicarius through the gritty maelstrom, eyes narrowed as the fine particles billowed around him. Emerging through the sandstorm, he thumped his plastron once in salute before delivering his report.

'A fourth ork fort lies to the east, across the gulch and further along the Blackwallow river,' he said, his voice clipped and with an icy undercurrent. 'It's isolated and well hidden. We only caught sight of it by chance, a light refraction from the structure's steel sidings. Initial reconnaissance indicates that a large ork of similar build and ostentation to the warlord is residing there. It could be your quarry, brother-captain.'

Sicarius nodded slowly, clapping the shoulder of the old veteran.

Scipio saw the underlying agitation vanish, the slightly obsessive demeanour that the captain had cultivated in the last few hours disappear in a blink. The hunter had his prey again.

'Haxis,' Sicarius said into his comm-feed, addressing his pilot, though his eyes were still on Telion. 'Engage the engines, we are leaving immediately. Brothers,' he added, looking around expansively, 'we go to hunt the ork.'

The greenskins fled, leaving the broken bodies of their kin behind them.

Thunder boomed in the heavens, but not from any storm. The Space Marine cannons were speaking, their blistering salvos ripping into the ork ranks as they scrambled desperately for the cover offered by the sparse petrified forests surrounding Ghospora.

Each Thunderfire cannon, meticulously deployed according to Captain Sicarius's precise instructions, rocked back on its tracks with a relentless, pounding rhythm, the quad barrels spitting out surface detonation shells with unerring regularity. Techmarine Lascar had performed his rites well.

It was the fifth assault in five days. Only on the first day had the orks been in a position to attack the bastion wall directly. Sergeant Tirian's devastator squad, coupled with punitive salvos from the Thunderfire cannons, had ended that threat prematurely. After that the greenskins hadn't even got close, and had been reduced to long-range shelling ever since.

'Do you think they'll return?' Praxor's voice came through on the comm-feed via Iulus's gorget. The sergeant noted the tone of hopeful expectation in his voice.

Iulus looked out over the smoking carnage, the explosive eruptions ripping up clods of earth and shredding ork bodies growing ever more distant. He raised his hand to indicate a cessation to the barrage.

'No, that last volley has broken them I think,' he replied once the storm was over. 'We could switch to airbursts and drive them from the trees but it would be a waste of munitions, and at extreme range... needlessly punitive.'

The comm-feed was still open. Iulus could hear the ambient noise from the other side of the rampart where Praxor was stationed with one of his combat squads.

Something was clearly on the sergeant's mind.

'Speak,' Iulus said.

There was a further moment's pause.

'There is no glory in this,' Praxor's response was flat.

'*They* are glad of it,' Iulus replied, referring to the Sable Gunners. 'They get to live their short and hurried lives a day or two longer at least.'

'Why did he leave us behind, Iulus?'

'Astartes were needed to hold on to what we had already gained, or would you have left Ghospora to its fate?' Praxor lowered his voice. Despite the fact the two sergeants conversed over a closed channel, he did not wish to be overheard.

'It may have held. And if not, it would have been a necessary sacrifice to find and kill the warlord, and save all of Black Reach.'

'And gain another laurel for our banner? What of the battle-brothers who died in the first assault, what of their sacrifice? Would you have that be in vain, Praxor?'

'No!' Praxor snapped louder. 'No,' he repeated, lowering his voice again, 'of course not...'

'Your question, brother, is why he left *you* behind, is it not?'

Praxor's silence answered for him.

'Perhaps it is because the High Suzerain values your experience in keeping what he has already won. Or perhaps he felt you needed to garner a stronger affinity for the human charges we protect. To me they are little more than instruments, no different to the steel of the walls or the shells in the heavy guns. But as I value this wall and those shells, I value them. You, my brother, do not.'

Praxor maintained his silence a little longer.

'I'll commence sweeps of the wall to see if any of the orks have escaped notice beneath our guns,' he replied curtly, cutting the comm-feed.

Praxor's irritation was obvious. His squad were experienced. They had fought in many Chapter-level campaigns, distinguishing themselves with honour, but they lacked compassion. Iulus did too, but that was due to his pragmatic nature, the way he dissembled flesh and blood into materiel.

Unlike Praxor, he was pleased. The defence had gone better than he could have hoped. Minimal casualties amongst the Sable Gunners, and none of the Astartes had been so much as wounded. Sicarius had planned well, and prudently. In truth, Iulus's siege expertise had not been needed. He had but to execute the strategy given.

In spite of himself, Iulus was forced to acknowledge his opinion of the captain was changing. He would die for him, obey his every command and fulfil it to his utmost – that had never been in question. But the doubts he had as to the High Suzerain's methods, his yearning for renown and standing amongst the Chapter, the desire to supplant venerable Agemman: that had changed.

Two such noble heroes in our midst...

Iulus recalled Scipio's words.

'You are ever with your quiet wisdom, eh brother?' Iulus muttered to himself.

Hurried movement along the rampart got his attention. Corporal Vormast's aide was approaching. His face was ashen.

'Sire,' he began, genuflecting and removing his helmet in an act of deference.

'Do not kneel to me, soldier. We are both warriors in the Emperor's service,' Iulus told him sternly. 'And never remove your helmet on the battlefield. It is worn for your protection, and not to be taken off to serve due deference.'

'Yes, my lord,' said the aide quickly, and stood up.

'Now, give me your report, Sable Gunner.'

'We have received distress calls,' said the aide, looking up at Iulus in awe and reverence despite the Ultramarine's chastisement. 'The orks are on the march. Sulphora Hive will be under attack in a matter of hours.'

The ork fort burned. Twisted metal and broken bodies lay chewed up in the earth. Gunfire raged. War cries – alien and Astartes – rent the air in a bellicose chorus.

Scipio ran through the carnage, the rest of the Thunderbolts, bereft of Hekor, behind him. A ramshackle hut near to their position, little more than a box crate festooned with armour plates and daubed glyphs, was struck by a slew of incendiary and exploded, showering the Space Marines with frag.

Through the lens capture in his new Astartes battle helm, Scipio saw a trio of greenskins toting rockets and high-calibre cannons stationed on the roof of a crude watchtower.

Tapping his gorget, Scipio spoke into the comm-feed.

'Up on the roof,' he barked, ducking as shell-fire strafed overhead and an errant rocket immolated an already burning ork truck, blasting out shrapnel. 'North-east corridor.'

'Neutralising…' was the curt response from Devastator Squad Atavian.

The foreboding retort of support weapons from the Titan Slayers boomed a moment later, and the watch tower was lit up like an incandescent candle by a ball of promethium. Heavy bolter rounds pummelled the blazing orkoid figures falling earthward from its destruction.

When Scipio's vision adjusted from the actinic blast, he saw that the tower had been reduced to a charred stump of smouldering metal. There was nothing left.

Sergeant Atavian was terse in his confirmation. 'Threat eliminated.'

The comm-feed was cut abruptly.

'Three down, only five hundred to go,' muttered Scipio cynically as he gave the order to move up and close with the enemy.

The dense cluster of ork buildings that comprised the fourth stronghold was surrounded by a dense wall of armour plate and corrugated siding. Cast iron braces reinforced the wall and were also driven into the scorched earth beyond, criss-crossed and welded into tank traps. The empty shells of large vehicles sat beyond the crude perimeter in small groups, some bolted together to form makeshift dwellings. The orks had also constructed box huts and hangars from steel sidings and scavenged sections of the Ghosporan bastion wall and its associated defences. They were rammed together behind the stronghold's delineating barrier, overlooked by ganglion watch towers, and formed streets, avenues and plazas as if in some crude mockery of civilisation. Tussocks of razor wire crowned the roof of each and every one; gun emplacements were ubiquitous throughout. Sandbags, ammo crates and stockpiles of naked munitions filled in gaps and added to the overtly militaristic milieu.

The attack had come at night. Eschewing the gate for a more oblique line of assault, Telion and his saboteurs had crept stealthily past the web of searchlights and reached the east-facing wall in under a minute. From there it had taken six seconds for the veteran sergeant and his scouts to blow a hole in the siding large enough for a Thunderhawk. Fourteen seconds more and the parapet sentries and two watch towers were neutralised in the flare of monochromatic muzzle flashes. Twelve more and the first-strike assault squads were through the breach in the ork defences and raising hell in the confusion. Another eighteen seconds and the orks started to mobilise their forces. That was when the Thunderhawks and the rest of the Astartes battle group tore over the ridge through the darkness. Less than two minutes and the Ultramarines were inside the fort, fighting amongst the avenues that were filling rapidly with blood.

Scipio heard the throb of turbofans behind him as *Pilium* screamed overhead. The whoosh and thrust of ordnance followed it a second later as the craft dumped a payload of Hellstrike missiles into a mass of greenskin armour approaching from the east. The detonation was thunderous, shaking the earth and tearing a great hole in the blackness. Fire plumes spewed from the immense incendiary and streamed in pyrotechnic glory as the orks were thrown into the air like ugly dolls, their machineries rendered to scrap.

'Drive on!' bellowed Veteran Sergeant Daceus, pointing with his bulky power fist to a contested plaza beyond the shelter of the huts where Scipio and his squad were waiting. 'Press them back. Herd them together for the Thunderhawks' missiles.'

He led the Lions of Macragge forward into a horde of clambering orks working their way through the wreckage done by *Pilium*. The rest of the gunships circled overhead like carrion, their pilots observing the battlefield through long-range sensor arrays, waiting for the orks to cluster before they ordered the gunners to unleash their missiles.

Scipio went in after Daceus, right on the heels of the Lions with Tactical Squads Solinus, Vandar and Octavian. Their bolters barked as one, stitching a lutescent firestorm across the no-man's-land between the Ultramarines and the advancing greenskins.

Scipio felt and heard bullets whine past his battle helm, shells *crump* overhead. Something hit his pauldron, but he shrugged it off and kept going. A battle-brother, he didn't see who, went down alongside him – another victim of the orks' custom cannons. The beasts were well equipped; this had to be Zanzag's mob.

A few metres from the onrushing greenskins, a wave of orks bearing burn-scars and wearing welding masks emerged from the horde. Their brutish hands were swathed in rags or covered by thick gloves, and they toted crude-looking flame throwers.

A blur of movement flashed overhead. With the scream of jump pack engines Squads Strabo and Ixion landed amidst the ork vanguard, cutting them down. Scipio saw Sicarius with them, a jump pack strapped to his artificer armour, rending with the Tempest Blade. The orks were shaken and on the back foot when Daceus and the other squads charged in. One lightning assault and the greenskins were falling back.

Scipio heard his captain barking down the comm-feed as the carnage raged. 'Sergeant Helios, are you in position?'

He paused for a beat, awaiting the Terminator's answer before replying.

'Good. Bring it to the west quadrant. We have the plaza and are moving there now.'

Clearing the armour wreckage with frag grenades, the combined battle group advanced, harrying the retreating orks all the way.

Daceus set up a fire-team with Squads Vandar and Octavian to guard the northern approach to the plaza through which the greenskins were fleeing. He had no desire to be outflanked by the foe if they found their courage and came back.

There was a greater mass of orks to the west of the stronghold, the warriors of Zanzag's clan. The bulk of the Ultramarines were heading straight for it, right into their jaws.

The greenskin elites were gathered in a veritable junkyard of trucks, wagons and buggies in the west quarter of the ork stronghold. The pintle-mounted armaments of the vehicles were still operational and being used as improvised gun emplacements. Stretching in front of the stronghold was a rolling mass of orks and orkoid armour. And there in the very centre – overlooking his mob in a crude crow's nest on one of the massive wagons – was Zanzag, cursing like a crazed priest.

Bolter fire hammered in the inky depths behind the massed greenskins – Helios and his Terminators, together with the dreadnoughts, forcing Zanzag to seek refuge in the middle of his horde. The ork thought it was safe surrounded by its kin. It had no concept of the danger it was in; Sicarius had it exactly where he wanted it.

'That's it Arcus,' he growled beneath his breath. 'Bring it to my teeth.'

'Into the jaws of hell, then,' remarked Daceus grimly, reunited with his captain once more, as he looked out across the endless green.

He was standing with the rest of the Lions, taking cover at the commencement of the ork shelling behind a cluster of barricades. The rest of the Ultramarines had moved into position around them and were returning the ork fire with determination.

'Not necessarily, brother,' Sicarius returned. 'We have but to sever the head,' he reminded him amidst the raucous din of the bolter storm: the Ultramarines were engaging.

'Yes, my captain,' Daceus agreed, 'and the head lies through that.'

'We have to outflank them, strike were the line in thinnest,' Sicarius told him. 'Hold the company here. Brother-Chaplain,' he added, as the skull-faced Orad appeared alongside the command squad. The Chaplain's crackling crozius seemed to echo his mood. 'You will assume operational command. Stymie the ork tide. Keep the beast's eye fixed on you.'

'And where will you be, brother-captain?' asked Daceus, evidently nonplussed by Sicarius's strategy.

A massive explosion rocked the left flank of the ork horde, deep within their lines. The resulting conflagration spread like a hungry wave, incinerating the orks in an ephemeral flame storm. Sporadic bolter fire ripped into the night in its wake from concealed positions, dull and distant.

Scipio was at the front line of the barricades alongside Sicarius and his Lions. They had engaged the greenskins at long-range. His bolt pistol was useless at this point so he watched the ork warlord instead, hollering at his troops to plug the burning hole in their ranks where Telion's explosion had gouged it.

'I will be exploiting the gap, sergeant,' he heard Sicarius reply.

'Sergeants Strabo and Vorolanus,' he continued, 'you and your squads are with me.'

Scipio's post at the barricade was taken up by Sergeant Octavian and his Swords of Judgement, as he and the Thunderbolts followed Captain Sicarius stomping over to the right flank with Strabo's assault squad.

'Assault squads are the vanguard,' said Sicarius curtly and efficiently as they made their way through scattered debris and burned out buildings in order to get into an outflanking position. 'Sergeant Vorolanus, you are our back-up.'

Scipio was about to acknowledge but quickly realised they were moving on at speed. His heart was pounding in his chest.

Led into battle by the Master of the Watch himself!

'Thunderbolts form up on my lead,' he said into the comm-feed, trying to keep pace.

Taking an oblique route around the main battle-front, slaying any greenskin stragglers as they found them, Scipio arrived at an immense hangar. Crossing the threshold a few seconds after Sicarius and Squad Strabo, the sergeant saw a small fleet of wrecked ork bombers. Fire lapped languidly over their fuselages, the craft long destroyed by Telion and his saboteurs.

Farther in there was more evidence of the scout sergeant's handiwork. Dead greenskin sentries – pilots, mechanics and gretchin slaves amongst them – littered the ground. Most had had their throats slit, though there were some with deep-bore blade wounds to their eyes and ears, or single-shot executions to their head. Experience fighting the greenskins had taught the Astartes that an ork's brain was small and compacted within thick layers of skull. It made such a kill-shot all the more impressive.

Sicarius was a glorious leader. He inspired and fought with the courage of Guilliman, even if his methods were capricious and unfathomable at times. But Telion was something else altogether. Scipio balked at the scout's prowess. He seemed to be everywhere at once, wreaking havoc, sowing discord like he stringed chains of incendiary. 'Dangerous' did not begin to describe him; even 'lethal' fell a way short.

Scipio had no time to consider it further – they had reached a dead end.

The back of the vast hangar was a steel-reinforced wall. Judging by the wear and crude graffiti, it must have been one of the first structures the greenskins had built upon touching down on Black Reach. Thick, iron stanchions supported it from the inside, and metal rebars were visible through the ferrocrete. Scipio doubted even Brother Agnathio could smash through it.

'Transmit our coordinates to the *Gladius*,' Sicarius ordered Sergeant Strabo.

The captain removed his helmet and clasped it to his battle-plate as Strabo relayed their position to the Thunderhawk.

'My lord, why are you removing your armour?' asked Scipio, briefly concerned that Sicarius's desire to slay the ork warlord had somehow dulled his good sense.

The captain smiled at him. His eyes glinted with inner fire.

'I want the beast to see my face as I kill it,' he explained. 'Never underestimate the effect this has on the enemy. It will see my wrath first hand, recognise that I do not fear it, and quail before me.'

Sicarius thumbed his gorget, accessing the comm-feed, once Strabo was done. 'Brother Haxis, we are ready,' he said, 'Make me a door.'

He closed the comm-feed and ordered them back twenty metres.

Scipio crouched behind a half-demolished wall, his squad arrayed around him.

'If he's doing what I think he's doing,' remarked Brother Garrik on a closed channel, 'then a missile strike from a gunship firing blind will have a margin of error of plus or minus twenty-five metres.'

'Then we had best hope that Brother Haxis flies true, and his gunner is accurate,' Scipio replied as the thrum of heavy engines approaching overhead rocked dust motes from the vaulted hangar ceiling.

The screech from the Hellstrike missile came a second later. A second after that and the hangar wall was blasted apart.

Debris was still falling when Sicarius was up and sprinting through the gaping hole left by the *Gladius's* precise attack.

Bent rebars jutted like metal bones and the stanchions was crushed and split before the concussive force of the explosion. Ferrocrete lay in chunks; thick dust cascaded like grey rain. Scipio barrelled through it all, he and his squad on the heels on Strabo.

The massive aperture punched through the wall led out into the heart of the greenskin horde. And as Scipio surged through it, killing awestruck orks as he went, he could hear the angered bellowing of Zanzag, and see him clearly in the wagon's tower.

Sicarius had seen him, too.

He was several metres ahead of the chasing Ultramarines, laying waste to anything in his path. Reaching a makeshift barricade of heaped trucks and wagons, Sicarius bounded up it thumbing his jump pack for extra loft.

Scaling the obstacle in seconds, ignoring the bullets pinging off his armour, he leapt from the very zenith of the crude vehicle tower. Despite their advantageous position, the distance between it and Zanzag's vantage point was vast.

An almost impossible jump.

Scipio whispered the name of Roboute Guilliman as his captain sprang over the churning sea of greenskins. An explosion blossomed in the darkness, throwing light onto his gleaming armour. He looked like an azure angel soaring through the bullet-ridden night, tracer rounds screaming around him.

Sicarius landed on the edge of the wagon tower, his heavy boots crushing the metal underfoot. Firing off a burst from his plasma pistol, the captain seared his enemy's torso, melting armour plate. Zanzag growled in pain, but shrugged off the blow and swung with his axe. Perched precariously on the tower, Sicarius would have fallen had he not deflected the attack with his power sword. Sparks spat from the blades in an ephemeral electrical storm as they met and parted in seconds.

Unperturbed, Zanzag swung again, only for Sicarius to smack the axe down with the flat of his sword and then trap it with his armoured boot. Before the greenskin warlord could recover, Sicarius lunged with the Tempest Blade, forcing the power sword through the beast's heaving chest. A gushet of blood spilled out as Sicarius withdrew the weapon before the wound cauterised. A second blow took off Zanzag's hand at the wrist as the ork fought to release his axe from beneath his foe's boot. The greenskin howled in rage, baring its teeth and promising retribution. Sicarius matched it with fury of his own.

Face fixed in a grimace of belligerence, and with his enemy stricken and mutilated, the Ultramarines captain swung his Tempest Blade and decapitated the warlord in one savage cut.

Zanzag's gruesome head fell from his shoulders and bounced into the thronging orks below. Sicarius kicked the still-flailing body down after it and roared his triumph.

A wave of disbelief swept over the orks. Their sudden distress was almost palpable. The infighting followed it immediately as rival chieftains sought to fill the power void.

Zanzag's minders, at first agog at the sudden slaying of their warlord, found their composure quickly and turned on Sicarius. The scar-veterans levelled their custom cannons, eager for revenge, but were swarmed by Strabo and his squad.

Scipio was right on the assault sergeant's heels with the Thunderbolts. Together they encircled the captain protectively, and held the orks at bay.

The main Ultramarines force was now in full attack. Chaplain Orad was audible over the battle-din, using his vox-unit like a loud hailer again as he spat liturgies of cleansing and hate-filled catechisms.

From the opposite direction, Sergeant Helios pressed with his inviolable Terminators and the mighty dreadnoughts Agnathio and Ultracius.

Caught between two determined foes, and with Telion and his scouts cutting a swathe through the heart of their ranks, the orks broke. Discord reigned as the greenskins started killing each other in a desperate bid to escape the Astartes' wrath.

None shall survive. That was Sicarius's decree. In the butchery that followed, the greenskins were slain to an ork.

Zanzag's dead eyes stared glassily into the encroaching dawn. Itinerant smoke drifted across the charnel fields where the head lay, disturbed by a fitful breeze carrying the stench of death.

A combat blade rammed unceremoniously into the decapitated cranium, and lifted it off the ground.

Telion crouched atop a carpet of strewn greenskin corpses, the slain carcass of the warlord amongst them. He'd used the body to locate the head.

Space Marines patrolled the battlefield in dispersed formations, executing injured greenskins, searching for the captain's prize. It had not been where Sicarius had dispatched it, having been carried off by some of its kin in some final bizarre act of reverence.

It was little wonder that Telion had found it first. Very little escaped the master scout's notice.

Scipio had been close, but the veteran sergeant had beaten him to it.

As he lifted the head to examine it, a tic of dissatisfaction manifested briefly in Telion's otherwise impassive expression.

Captain Sicarius, having noticed the master scout's find, had moved into his vicinity.

'This is not the beast,' said Telion, stoically.

Sicarius's eyes narrowed in displeasure. 'Are you sure?' It was an utterly pointless question, asked in hope rather than expectation.

'See here,' said the veteran sergeant, pulling back the dead ork's lip. 'A full set of tusks, no recent wounding.'

Sicarius had stung the beast at Ghospora, shooting its neck and jaw. There was no evidence of such an injury on the head Telion held forth on his blade.

'Trappings, size, mass – it's almost a perfect analogue,' said the scout. 'Such cunning is rare in the greenskin.'

'What do you mean, brother-sergeant?' asked Scipio, similarly drawn by Telion's discovery.

'I mean that this was planned. The orks created an imperfect doppelganger.'

'But to what end? What purpose could such a thing serve?'

Sicarius answered. The hardness in his expression that was there on the sandblasted clearing in the corral of Thunderhawks had returned.

'To lick its wounds, gather the strength of its horde for another assault. This way they wear us down, take us away from where we are needed most, and thin our ranks,' he said. 'We Ultramarines are more than a match for any ork, but our numbers are few in comparison. In a war of attrition, the greenskin hold the advantage,' Sicarius conceded.

The Blackwallow flowed nearby. Sicarius eyed it darkly as if trying to catch a glimpse of something just beyond his reach. 'And now we must do it all again,' he said.

Veteran Sergeant Daceus tramped across the killing field, his face grimmer than usual, good eye as blank and cold as the bionic. He saluted tersely before he spoke.

'A message has come in via the *Gladius*, my lord,' he said. 'The orks are moving on Sulphora Hive.'

The captain clenched his armoured fist, the gauntlet creaking under the stress. 'Telion, continue the search for the ork. Perhaps a subtler approach is needed to draw it out.' Turning to Daceus, he said: 'The rest of the battle group will head for Sulphora.'

The veteran sergeant nodded and went off to organise the troops.

'I'm a scout squad down,' said Telion. 'Reinforcements will be needed for what I have in mind.'

Sicarius turned to Scipio who was just about to gather the Thunderbolts. 'Sergeant Vorolanus, your squad specialises in reconnaissance and deep-strike operations, yes?'

'Yes, my lord.'

'Pick four of your best, send the others to Daceus to cover casualties in the other squads. You're with Brother-Sergeant Telion now.'

'You wish to break up my squad?' To question a superior was insubordinate, but Scipio could not believe what he was hearing. He meant no disrespect by the remark.

'For the good of the Chapter, select your brothers and Daceus will take care of the rest.' Sicarius's tone made it clear he would brook no debate.

'Yes, brother-captain,' answered Scipio, nodding his head in penance and respect.

As Sicarius turned on his heel and stalked away, Scipio's gaze drifted over to Telion.

The master scout's face was utterly unreadable. 'Welcome to the 10th, Sergeant Vorolanus,' he said without a trace of humour.

Scipio met the icy glare of Telion with one of his own. He'd lost Hekor already; his body would be cooling in the mortarium aboard the *Valin's Revenge*. Now, four more were being taken in the name of slaying Zanzag and getting the captain his prize. The Thunderbolts had been torn apart.

Scipio's response was terse.

'What are your orders, Sergeant Telion?'

The night was quiet; identical, in fact, to the previous night. The distant retort of heavy guns as the battle for Sulphora was fought came over on the breeze like thunder. As he stared into the dark, surrounded by a copse of petrified trees in the lay of the Blackwallow River, Scipio imagined the fire-orange explosions, the powder-white smoke plaguing the walls as the defence artillery vented. His brothers, one half of his squad, fought in that combat whilst he surveilled a ruin.

'South-east approach quadrant one, clear,' he spoke

softly into the comm-bead attached to his armour
and which fed into his ear.

Upon selecting his battle-brothers, Scipio and the
four members of his squad had been instructed to
report to the *Xiphos* at once. There, they had been
divested of their power armour and clad in the
armoured carapace of the scout company, the former deemed too loud and cumbersome for the
covert operation Telion had in mind. The process
had been swift, even though the Thunderhawk had
lingered long after the other gunships. It would join
the others later at Sulphora. Chaplain Orad had
voiced concerns over the lack of proper observance
during the removal of the battle-brothers' power
armour, but Sicarius was adamant that it be done.
Every measure must be taken to find the beast, and
taken quickly.

In the end, Orad had no choice but to concede.
Waiting behind with *Xiphos* and an honour guard
of Squad Octavian, he gave a curt blessing and Telion's latest recruits were made ready.

The unfamiliar sensation of the lighter armour left
Scipio feeling exposed and uncomfortable as Garrik's
report came back echoing his own – no movement
in quadrant two, either.

The two five-man squads were widely dispersed
around the full perimeter of the wrecked ork stronghold. Every angle of approach was covered. The
Astartes waited silently in concealed positions. Telion reasoned that the orks would return to loot and
scavenge. It was in their nature. The Ultramarines had
only to make them believe that they had abandoned

the ruins in favour of the war zone at Sulphora. As of yet, their prey had not bitten.

A red scorpion, indigenous to Black Reach, scuttled towards him, its barbed tail poised to strike. Scipio impaled it on his combat blade before releasing the stricken insect and crushing it beneath his boot. Frustration from inactivity was starting to get the better of him, and for a moment he caught a glimpse into the self-same feelings of his captain.

'How much longer must we wait, cowering in the dark?' Scipio muttered to himself.

'As long at it takes, brother.'

Scipio started at the voice of Telion, instinct making him reach for his bolt pistol.

'You have fast reactions,' Telion noted, creeping up alongside him. The veteran sergeant was utterly soundless as he moved. Even Scipio's advanced hearing had failed to detect his approach.

'My apologies, brother-sergeant,' Scipio replied.

Telion moved almost imperceptibly in what might have been a shrug.

'It's patient work. You're used to the roar and thrust of the battlefield now. Adjustment is never easy. The hardest time for a warrior is when he is at rest.' Telion kept his eyes on the Blackwallow as he spoke, his stalker-pattern boltgun with its shortened stock and targeter cradled loosely in his lap. The effect was disarming, but in truth, Scipio knew, Telion was in a state of absolute readiness. Whenever he adopted that veneer of calm was when the master scout was at his most dangerous.

Silence descended for a beat, broken only by the

gentle flow of the river, and the droning of cicada and the other chitinous native species of Black Reach skittering across displaced sand.

'You trained him, didn't you,' said Scipio, wanting to dispel some of the tension but also trusting Telion enough to engage his opinion.

'I trained many of the captains of the Chapter, as I have done numerous Chapters,' Telion replied, understanding immediately what Scipio was driving towards.

'I saw him at Ghospora. He was magnificent. His heroism and courage seems to have no limits.'

Telion stayed silent, inviting Scipio to continue.

'It was no different at the fort. But there was a moment... a moment when I thought hubris would get the better of him.'

'You refer to the bravura attack that single-handedly broke the will of the horde,' Telion interjected. 'I saw it, too.'

If there was any implication in Telion's words then Scipio did not detect it.

'If he had failed that jump, he would likely be dead and our victory would not have been as easy, if in fact guaranteed at all,' Scipio asserted, trying to choose his next words carefully. 'It seemed... fraught with risk.'

Telion went silent again for a beat, as if contemplating.

'We are all guilty of hubris, Brother Vorolanus. The mere fact we campaign the length of the galaxy to ensure mankind's dominance of it is proof of that. And risk? Risk is only equal to reward, and at the stronghold the reward was great.

'I have never sought the trappings of glory, though

the honours bequeathed to me by my captains and my Chapter Masters are many. But I understand the *need* for heroes. Not those that skulk around in the dark or forge iron-hard warriors from the soft clay of neophytes, but visible heroes who will see glory for what it is and seize it. On such things are the foundations of our Chapter built.'

Now it was Scipio's turn to fall silent. Telion was right, of course. His wisdom was centuries old, and it showed. Any reply of gratitude, though, was forestalled by the master scout's raised hand.

Slowly, he nodded towards the dormant surface of the Blackwallow.

Scipio followed his eye-line.

'Something comes,' he hissed, and crouched down further into the petrified trees.

Scipio followed suit, watching as a dense cluster of bubbles rose to the surface of the cloying water, discreet at first but then developing rapidly into an almighty emergence. An array of antennas and exhausts burst from the churning depths, closely followed by a jagged metal fin shearing through the surface of the wide river. A dense black hull, thick with armour plating and glyphs, emerged after that. Piping and circular portholes punctuated the sides of the vessel's bulky body. Dorsal gun mounts cascaded with dark water as they surfaced. A brutal-looking propulsion motor squatted at the vessel's aft, slowing to a stop as it finished blowing ballast in order to rise. Scipio, a veteran ork hunter who knew something of their debased language, read a crude appellation on its nearside in ork glyph script: *Morkilus*.

The mystery surrounding how the greenskins launched their lightning assaults and disappeared without trace was solved – they had a submersible.

After a periscope had probed the surrounding area for potential threats, a series of hatches opened in the submersible's roof, and a dozen orks and over three times that number of gretchin pooled out. They grunted to one another in their debased language. One ork, his head and torso protruding from the hatch, wore a large, battered hat and chewed on a cigar. He cuffed one of the gretchin around the ear for some slight before disappearing back into the lumpen vessel and slamming the hatch shut.

The scouts waited patiently in the shadow of the trees until the entire greenskin landing party had entered the ruins of the stronghold. Only a pair of gretchin remained on the surface outside the vessel, yanking at the pipe work and battering down bent armour plates with oversized wrenches and hammers.

Telion gave a sub-vocal command over the comm-bead, signalling for the scouts to hold position and maintain overwatch. Using Astartes battle-sign, he then told Scipio what would happen next.

The submersible had emerged in their quadrant, therefore he and Telion would prosecute the mission. Both Space Marines trod silently from their concealed positions in the petrified trees, eyes fixed on the bickering gretchin.

As he stalked towards his prey, Scipio lost sight of Telion, the master scout blending into the surrounding darkness. Five metres from the gretchin crew and one of them turned. Scipio's blood froze and he was about to throw his combat blade when the diminutive greenskin jolted and a puff of crimson ejected from its ear. Its cousin reacted to the sudden movement, eyes wide when it saw the Ultramarine. Its mouth was sketching a scream when a silenced *thwit* came from the dark, and it suffered the same fate as its kin.

Scipio moved past the corpses at once. His instructions were clear, relayed to him before surveillance had begun. Reaching the bank of the river, he waded slowly into the water. It was chill as it seeped through his fatigues and armour.

Guiding himself around the hull, using the armour plating for purchase, his body flat against it so as to limit his exposure, Scipio worked his way to the nose. Once there, he let go of the plating and allowed himself to sink beneath the surface. His multi-lung let him breathe the water like air, though he wasn't down in the Blackwallow's depths for long enough to need it.

Feeling for a pouch on his combat belt, Scipio produced a small tracer and fixed it to the under-side of the hull. Once he was certain the device was operative, he swam back up to the surface. The sound of raucous looting was carried to him on the breeze. The orks were still busy. As he got to the bank again, Scipio noticed that the gretchin corpses had already gone. There were no tracks, no sign of them ever having been present. It was as if they had simply disappeared. Likely the orks would think so too, if they even noticed they were gone at all.

Once he was back in hiding, Scipio simply waited.

Morning sun spilled over the sand dunes of Black Reach like a fiery veil. The petrified trees cast long and jagged shadows against its brilliance. The Black-wallow flowed quietly, dormantly – the moored submersible was gone. Earlier in the night, the orks had returned from their scavenging, boarded and left. Hatches were slammed shut, the dead gretchin were not missed and the submersible had filled its tanks and plunged back beneath the river.

'The tracer beacon is working,' said Telion, standing at the edge of the forest. Garrik was alongside him and held up an auspex for the veteran-sergeant's perusal. Scipio stood with them both.

'The signal terminates at the cliff face where the river reaches its end,' Telion said, after a moment.

'How can we be sure it was Zanzag's vessel?' Scipio asked.

'We can't,' admitted Telion, 'which is why we have these.' He held up the two dead gretchin he had executed like a hunter with a brace of vermin.

'We only need one,' he added, dropping a gretchin to the ground before ordering Garrik to hide the other in the trees.

Kneeling next to the corpse, Telion drew his combat blade and made a deep incision in the gretchin's skull. First, he cut away the skin and flesh, then he used the combat blade's pommel to crack the bone and break open the skull. He dipped his fingers through the crevice, reaching for the gooey mass of matter encased within. He then consumed it and closed his eyes.

A Space Marine's omophagea was situated between the thoracic vertebrae and the stomach wall. For the more poetically inclined, it was named the Remembrancer, as it allowed Astartes who consumed the flesh and organs of any creature to absorb part of that creature's memory. Delving into an alien psyche in this way was always dangerous, but gretchin were not possessed with the same unpredictable energy as orks; the experience could be controlled.

Telion's lids flickered, the rapid eye movement beneath an indication that the process of assimilation had begun. A few seconds passed and the master scout's face contorted in a grimace. He bared his teeth, jaw locked in concentration. Images would be flooding his mind, impressions garnered from the gretchin's primitive neural pathways. From this melange of sensations – sight, sound, smell, touch and taste – Telion would build a mental picture, using his advanced Astartes physiology to sift and sort memory strands into cognisance, into meaning.

Scipio and the other Astartes looked on stoically, knowing not to intervene, but to let the process take its course. In spite of that, the tension was still palpable.

Sweat beaded the master scout's forehead. Telion clenched his fists as he continued to probe, to ransack the genetic matter he had ingested, manipulate the chromosomal information implanted there and convert it into something he could use and understand.

After what seemed like many long minutes had passed, but in actuality was only a few seconds, Telion exhaled a calming breath and relaxed. When he opened his eyes again, he allowed himself a rare smile.

'Make contact with Captain Sicarius at once,' he told Scipio. 'Tell him we have found the beast's lair.'

PHASE FOUR – SLAY THE BEAST

Iulus cranked a round into the breech of his bolt pistol and smiled grimly at his battle-brothers.

His squad, the Immortals, were sitting around their sergeant, secured in their battle-harnesses in the troop hold of a Rhino APC. The bulky, slat-nosed vehicle ground on thick tracks over the shifting Black Reach sands at full throttle. Engines gunned to maximum bellowed through the metal hull, the troop hold rattling vigorously with the resonance. The Space Marines exhibited no distress, having undertaken numerous similar hell-for-leather deployments before.

They had left Ghospora Hive four hours previously and were hurtling at full speed as soon as they'd passed the gate. Once the message that Sulphora was under attack had been conveyed to Captain Sicarius,

Iulus and his squad were ordered to the defence of Ghospora's sister hive immediately. Praxor, as the officer in charge and with all the siege deterrents in place, was to remain behind, much to the sergeant's chagrin. It seemed to Iulus that Praxor's views about their captain were changing too.

Iulus gave them no heed; to him, one battlefield was much the same as another.

'How close are we to the gate, Brother Glavius?' he asked the driver through the Rhino's internal comm-feed.

The response was crackly and fraught with static. Glavius sounded slightly preoccupied. 'Approximately three thousand metres, sir.'

'How far are the greenskins from the wall?' Iulus continued, amber strip lights washing his bald pate and limning his armour.

'Approximately two thousand three hundred metres.'

'Then we had best make haste.'

'Yes, sir.'

Iulus cut the link and turned to his battle-brothers. 'Are you ready for hell again, my Immortals?' he asked them.

'Aye!' the response was resounding and in unison.

'Courage and honour,' Iulus growled, and his warriors echoed him.

Disengaging his harness so he could stand and reach for the fire point in the roof, Iulus muttered, 'Let's see what we're facing...'

The sergeant threw open the Rhino's top hatch, allowing light, air and dust to flood in. Squinting as he hooked up his rebreather mask, Iulus stood up fully and emerged from the fire point.

Over two kilometres out, Sulphora loomed like a jagged, black knife rammed into the crust of the planet. The sun was high in an ochre sky and threw harsh red light onto every facing surface, casting it in the hue of blood. Defence lasers and battle cannons emplaced on the walls shrieked and boomed in unison, the tremors reaching the Rhino all the way across the sand plain. Small-arms fire and heavier support guns rippled along ramparts and atop watch towers.

Though smaller than its neighbour, Sulphora was almost a carbon copy of Ghospora Hive, flash moulded into existence by an unimaginative engineer or mason-artisan, pock-marking Black Reach's surface just like all the others.

An immense gate loomed ahead, stark and prosaic. The flat, black slab of buttressed metal was grinding open slowly on immense gears. The Rhino would only need a crack to slip through.

'Magnoculars,' Iulus ordered, reaching down into the troop hold and coming up with the device in his hand. He surveyed the upcoming battle theatre through the scopes. Sable Gunners regiments were thin here, too. There were many gaps along the walls, gun emplacements unmanned and abandoned. But there was something else too; something that Ghospora had not had during its initial time of need – Space Marines. The brilliant blue armour of the Ultramarines shone as they moved along parapets, organised the native troops or made ready with cannons of their own. It would be good to rejoin the company, Iulus thought. He hoped to fight alongside Scipio again.

Panning to the east, Iulus saw the foe at once. The greenskins had massed a sizeable force, their own artillery spitting back against the Sulphoran guns. Brutish bikes and ramshackle wagons conveyed the horde, more ork dreadnoughts and the ubiquitous footsloggers marching in their wake.

'Alien scum,' Iulus cursed. 'You just don't know when you're beaten.'

The sergeant ducked down again, handing back the magnoculars, and sealed the fire point hatch. 'Brother Glavius...' he said into the comm-feed once he was back in his battle-harness.

'Eight hundred metres, sir.'

Iulus cut the link again, addressed his battle-brothers. 'Thirty seconds.'

Thirty seconds, he thought. It was going to be tight.

The Rhino screamed through the gate of Sulphora Hive and slewed to halt. Smoke was still issuing off the track axles when the rear and side hatches opened and Iulus and the Immortals piled out.

The heavy gate thundered shut behind them, the sentry crews working double time on the gears to seal it before the ork assault hit.

The hive interior was frantic with activity, ammunition couriers scurrying back and forth with manual haulers brimming with shells and belt feeds. Sable Gunner officers shouted orders from ramparts. Regiments of troops mustered up stairways and along battlements. Watch towers and emplacements were manned and made ready.

Amidst it all, Iulus watched as a Thunderhawk gun-ship descended from the sky, a gunmetal landing pad clearing for its descent.

Iulus approached the vessel while its turbofans were still whirring to a halt. The embarkation ramp lowered and Chaplain Orad stepped out with Squad Octavian.

'Report to Veteran Sergeant Daceus,' he barked at Iulus when he saw him, before marching off to mar-shal another part of the defence.

'Brother-Chaplain...' Iulus ventured.

Orad turned and fixed the sergeant with a glare through his skull-helm. To anyone other than Iulus, the effect would have been disconcerting.

'Sergeant Vorolanus – is he with the muster at Sulphora?'

'Your brother has been seconded into Brother-Sergeant Telion's service.' The Chaplain offered no further expla-nation as he continued about his business.

At least he is still alive, thought Iulus to himself, and went off in search of Daceus.

'Lower quadrant wall,' said Veteran-Sergeant Daceus, shouting to be heard over the assault. 'The Sulpho-ran defenders are weakest there.'

Iulus saluted and was about to get on his way when an urgent message came in through Daceus's comm-feed. The veteran-sergeant had a finger to his ear, opening the feed, and crouched behind the bat-tlements to better block out the surrounding clamour.

'Belay that order, Sergeant Fennion,' he barked.

'Sir?'

'Convene at the landing pad immediately,' he said. 'We are taking the *Gladius* and the *Pilium*.' A look of belligerent satisfaction grew over the Ultramarine's features. 'By Guilliman, Telion has found the beast's lair.'

The greenskin sentry struggled and then went limp as its life-blood oozed from its severed jugular vein.

Scipio hooked his arms underneath its brawny body and dragged the creature out of sight behind a scattering of boulders.

Flying their land speeders in low, the scouts had reached the submersible's destination swiftly. From the air, they had traced the long oily line of the Blackwallow until reaching its terminus at the edge of the granite cliff. From there the river peeled off into a wide and thrashing waterfall. Grey foam erupted where the falling water pooled in a shallow basin below, surrounded by a black boulder field wretched with harsh scrub and other resilient desert foliage.

The cliff face itself was almost sheer. There were few holds and the rocks were smooth and slick with pressure erosion. In places ragged spikes thrust out like rotten teeth, sharp enough to shear carapace. Any climb would be perilous. Telion, on his stomach as he had peered over the edge, had mapped a route in less than a minute. On his advance reconnaissance he had also counted four sentry points, viewed in detail through the magnoculars, set around the base of the waterfall. The orks were well hidden, spread in pitted craters and had scopes of their own. Runtish greenskin slaves carried messages back and forth across the boulder field like pendulums between them. Telion's suspicions had been raised when he saw one disappear behind the flowing curtain of water, only to remerge a few moments later on the other side.

The speeders had touched down a kilometre out, approaching from the south, out of the greenskins' immediate line of sight. The scout squads, one led by Telion, the other by Scipio with half of the Thunderbolts, had trekked over the boulder-strewn sand on two divergent routes. They'd reached the edge of the concealed ork camp at opposite ends of the waterfall and proceeded to stalk their way through the boulder field, taking out the sentries as they went.

The greenskin warlord had kept his outer guards light. Just three orks and six gretchin occupied each of the four vantage points. Any more would have been too difficult to conceal effectively and would be more likely to arouse suspicion. Zanzag was cautious as well as cunning, it seemed.

The scouts worked through the sentries systematically, neutralising them covertly with blades and silenced rounds. They moved swiftly, like shadows along the narrow passes through the rocks. Only when they reached the very edge of the falls and the last of the sentry points did an ork see them approaching. It was about to alert its kin when it realised they were already dead: one choking on its own blood with a combat blade lodged in its neck, the other face down in the dirt with an oozing head wound.

Telion put a round through its throat at fifty metres, closed and put two more through its head at twenty whilst at a run.

The two scout squads were reunited at the final sentry point before the ork had hit the ground. Now close to the bottom of the cliff face, the scouts could clearly see a wide crevice, large enough for an aircraft, concealed by the black torrent.

The crash of the waterfall blotted out sound as effectively as an engine baffler, so Telion battle-signed for them to enter in single file.

Scipio reciprocated the order to his squad and, with bolt pistol readied, they penetrated the curtain of water and went into the gloom beyond.

The scouts entered a vast natural tunnel. Thin rivulets of dark liquid flowed along the ground between them as they hugged the walls either side, using natural alcoves for cover. Now they were further away from the waterfall it was easier to detect noise and commotion coming from ahead. Light issued through a roughly hewn aperture at the tunnel's end. Two large ork bodies cradling custom cannons were framed in it. Scipio could smell their foetid stink on the air.

Telion battle-signed for the scouts to stop. They obeyed immediately, keeping to the shadows, as unmoving as statues. The master scout then went ahead, treading silently.

There was a distance of fifty metres between the ork guards and the waiting Space Marine scouts. Scipio lost sight of Telion after five. The next time he saw him, the master scout had stabbed the first greenskin in the neck and loomed before the second. Upon seeing the vengeful form of Telion, the ork was about to cry out but was prevented by a savage punch that snapped its hyoid bone. Enraged, the beast swept a meaty fist at the Ultramarine, but Telion ghosted from the blow's path and landed one of his own to its jaw. Spitting blood and sputum, one claw clutching its ruined neck, the ork went for its custom cannon. The master scout stepped within its reach, disarming it, before reversing his attack and slipping his blood-slick combat blade through the creature's chin and up into its brain. It shuddered once before slumping dead. Grimacing with the effort of carrying the brute, Telion laid the ork down then moved over to the other and double-tapped it with his silenced bolter through the skull, just to be sure. His work done, he beckoned the scouts onward.

The tunnel opened out in a massive cavern. The rock here, much like that of the cliff, was worn smooth by the constantly trickling rivulets of water peeling down the sides. They collected on a massive field of stalactites protruding from the vaulted ceiling, and dripped downwards like reluctant rain. The run-off gathered in craters that pock-marked the raised sedimentary platforms around the edges of the cavern. Ambient light refracted from luminescent mineral deposits, veining the rugged rock like streaks of marble.

Scipio could see further mineral strains flashing farther back into the gloom that suggested unseen depths, possibly even a cave system. The cavern was the major organ of that system, its tunnels its arteries. And it was immense, easily large enough to hold an entire fighter squadron from a strike cruiser – large enough, in fact, to hold an army.

Scipio guessed that the vast cavern had been formed naturally, drained over time and then expanded by orkish ingenuity. The Blackwallow flowed over the cliff face and into this very chamber before wending eastwards to the Sable Sea. It collected in a vast, dark lagoon in front of them.

It was deep, much deeper than the Astartes had first realised. The orks had directed it into six parallel channels, a crude concourse of ferrocrete alongside each one. Scipio balked when he saw what was moored in each of the channels: submersibles. Some underground channel must link the lagoon to the main stretch of the river, its pervasive tributaries allowing unparalleled and clandestine access to most of the planet.

A fat promethium line stretched down one side of the chamber and ran on into the unknown darkness beyond. The orks had tapped the subterranean reserve and must be using it to fuel their vehicles. It appeared that the *Morkilus* was just a sixth of the greenskins' maritime strength.

Scipio used his magnoculars to survey the vessels more closely.

They were all of a similar basic design with the usual anarchic flourishes the greenskins favoured.

Each one bristled with guns and had names like *Ork-tober*, *Dak Bork*, *Gorkliath*, *Tinteef* and *Sharky* written in glyph script. It appeared the orks were creative in their madness.

The half-dozen subs were arrayed in a busy docking station where scores of bent-backed gretchin loaders bustled back and forth with tools, drums and crates. Scipio panned the magnoculars further up the cavern, and saw that larger greenskins moved amongst the runts, low-slung stubbers draped over their broad shoulders. Scipio recognised the cigar-smoking ork from the previous night's surveillance. It was inspecting a cache of weapons in a steel ammunition crate marked with the Imperial eagle: weapons 'liberated' from the defeated hives no doubt.

Beyond the docking strips, the cavern opened out still further into a huge expanse of ferrocrete. Here was where the bulk of the greenskins gathered. There were thousands: drinking, brawling, gambling; some throttled their runtish cousins out of sadistic pleasure, others discharged weapons into the air seemingly at random, bellowing and roaring with bestial mirth.

More racks of weapons and munitions crates stacked at the fringes of the ferrocrete plaza were being tested and tinkered with by what appeared to be some form of orkoid mechanic or engineer. The greenskins were obviously planning a major offensive. The architect of it all, their grand warlord Zanzag, sat at the very end of the chamber.

Numerous ammo crates and fuel drums had been lashed together to form a makeshift throne.

There, Zanzag presided over his charges like a king. Gretchin slave runts hurried around him, fulfilling his every whim, whilst an ork in a blood-stained smock and carrying a fat syringe performed some kind of brutal surgery upon the warlord. The beast's broad back, criss-crossed with two black belts festooned with knives and cleavers, obscured Scipio's view, but the Ultramarine thought he caught the flash of a razor-saw before he lowered the magnoculars.

Crude sodium lighting rigs had been erected in the chamber, thick cables looped from each unit pressure-bolted into the vaulted cavern ceiling. They spat sparks intermittently, and offered feeble illumination. The scouts used it to their advantage, making their way stealthily into the cavern. Silently, they slid into the lagoon, navigating around the raised edges split into two squads. With just their eyes and the tops of their heads above the water-line, the scouts arrived at the busy dock, climbed up onto the ferrocrete and took cover amongst the clutter.

Every scout carried a belt of six krak grenades.

Scipio eyed the nearest submersible, the *Orktober*.

They wouldn't have long before Sicarius and the rest of 2nd Company arrived – they had to work quickly.

Scipio returned silently to his hiding place with an empty grenade belt. He secured a tiny palm-sized detonator in his webbing and waited. The ork surgeon had finished its ministrations and, as it stepped back, Scipio saw Zanzag clearly for the first time. The warlord was massive. Huge armoured guards full of spikes were strapped to his brawny shoulders. A jaw plate was bolted over his maw; the crude stitching overlaid old scar-tissue and was still visible running down the beast's neck. Its red eyes were set into a mutilated face wretched with rings and studs, and narrowed with malign intelligence.

It appeared the warlord had given up its power axe, as one of its arms was now encased in some kind of power claw, not unlike the one carried by the dreadnought Scipio had fought on the fields of Ghospora. The device snapped impatiently, pneumatics hissing, as if eager for blood. In his other hand, the beast clutched one of the customised cannon, though this one was larger and more unfathomably elaborate than the others Scipio had seen. The warlord rested the gun on his lap like a favoured pet, whilst a gretchin with unfeasibly large ears held up a polished piece of scrap like a mirror so that Zanzag could inspect the surgeon's handiwork.

The warlord regarded its reflection for a few moments before snarling and cuffing the runt to the ground. Zanzag was about to kick it when the entire cavern started to shake. Clods of grit and rock cascaded from the ceiling, and the sodium rigs flickered intermittently as if in warning.

Zanzag stooped, hoisted the big-eared gretchin by its neck and thrust it forwards, barking some unintelligible command.

The creature listened intently, shrugged and opened

its mouth to speak when its head exploded, spattering the warlord with gore.

Zanzag threw the headless gretchin to the ground, roaring to his followers.

Too late.

Gladius surged into the cavern like a blade, hull dripping water from where it had cut through the waterfall. Heavy bolters spoke, and the word was death. Ripping up orks as they clambered for weapons and for cover, the gunship launched a payload of Hellstrike missiles. A group of ork dreadnoughts mobilising at the back of the chamber was destroyed in the ensuing conflagration.

Hovering over the lagoon, the down thrust of its engines whipping the water into foam, the *Gladius* scattered greenskins with its guns, making a landing zone on one of the ferrocrete strips. The orks tried desperately to retaliate, firing off their custom cannons with abandon, but their crude science had not reckoned with the armour of a Thunderhawk, and the shots ricocheted away harmlessly.

As if in response, the artillery mounted on the submersibles cranked around noisily, trying to draw a bead on the deadly Astartes vessel. Before a shell was expelled, the six submarine war engines exploded, the krak grenades secreted about their hulls detonated by Scipio and his unseen brothers. The monstrous vehicles went up in a chain of explosions, spitting shrapnel like hard-edged rain in all directions as fire swept voraciously through and over them.

Confusion pervaded as the orks struggled to fight a foe that seemed to be everywhere at once. In a few short but frenzied seconds, the gunship had landed and its ramp was down. Roaring the name of the Chapter Master, Captain Sicarius surged out of the hold with his Ultramarines, bolters blazing. They rushed the concourse and gained an instant foothold.

Scipio ran from cover, adding his own shots to the unfolding battle, as more scouts emerged from across the cavern.

Zanzag was bellowing madly for order. The warlord shot three fleeing orks dead before the rest got the message and turned to fight. He grunted to his captains, and a mob of rocket-toting greenskins emerged out of the throng. Their ordnance whooshed on coal-black contrails and exploded around the *Gladius*, leaving the gunship's hull smouldering. Having disembarked its cargo, the Thunderhawk withdrew out of the cavern.

'Death from above, brothers!' bellowed Sicarius as he charged up the lane of ferrocrete, the burning wrecks of submersibles either side.

From the flickering gloom the warriors of Strabo descended and fell amongst the ork heavy weapons, slaying with chainswords and pistols. The sergeant himself gutted one beast with his power sword, whilst shooting into the face of another. The corpses slid off the concourse and into the inky void of the lagoon below.

With the fall of the rocket launchers, a second wave of greenskins bullied its way forward – more of Zanzag's scar-veterans with their custom cannons.

Strabo and his warriors took flight, jump packs pluming fire and smoke. Through the grey-black miasma emerged the Terminators of 1st Company, led by the indomitable Arcus Helios.

'In the name of Agemman and the Chapter,' he bellowed metallically through his battle helm as the orks let rip with their weapons. The Terminators were engulfed in a veritable storm of bullets but emerged unscathed, shots deflecting off their formidable armour like tin hail. In return, Squad Helios unleashed their storm bolters and cut a swathe through the greenskins. The orks desperately increased their rate of fire but to no avail. By the time they realised their weapons were ineffectual against the thickly armoured Astartes, dozens of greenskins were dead.

Balking at the indestructible warriors, many of the orks began to flee. Some dived into the black lagoon; others ran into the guns of their kin as they tried in vain to save their own miserable lives.

Arcus Helios and his brothers forged ahead, unstoppable.

Sicarius pressed the advantage. With most of the custom cannons eliminated, he signalled a full attack.

Scipio caught a glimpse of Iulus, urging his Immortals on as he joined the push with the captain. The orks were shaken but still numerous and met the charge with fury. Blood washed across the concourse as the two bitter enemies fought, paying for every metre won with pain and death.

Scipio found his way to the front, chainsword singing a bloody chorus as he killed.

'You truly walk amongst heroes, Sergeant Vorolanus,' said a familiar voice that could only be Iulus's, from alongside him.

'Aye, Sergeant Fennion,' Scipio replied, blasting an ork off the concourse with a controlled burst of fire, 'you amongst them.'

'Indeed, I am,' Iulus returned, shredding a kamikaze gretchin in mid-flight with his chainsword and coating his armour with its chewed up viscera.

'And a modest one at that.'

Overhead, the heavy *chunk* of Brother Ultracius's assault cannon could be heard as the dreadnought tore up the hapless greenskins with impunity.

Iulus laughed, wiping away a swathe of blood from his face with the back of his gauntlet. 'For the primarch!' he roared suddenly, in unison with his battle-brothers.

The orks were breaking.

Punching through a meagre rearguard, the Ultramarines emerged onto the ferrocrete expanse. Isolated mobs of greenskins remained, taking snap shots from behind crates and drums. Ultracius eviscerated one group, tearing apart their cover and igniting it in a fiery explosion. Assault Squad Strabo plunged on top of another, crushing runts beneath their armoured boots, whilst cleaving their orkish masters with their bolts and blades.

Captain Sicarius was heedless of all of it. He barrelled headlong across the ferrocrete. Solid shot pinged off his clanking armour as he made for an opening at the rear of the chamber. Scipio followed him with Iulus and his Immortals close behind.

Zanzag had fled again, using the network of caves at the back of the vast cavern to make his escape.

Twice now the beast had eluded the Ultramarines

in one fashion or another. There would not be a third.

'Face me, beast!' yelled Sicarius, his challenge echoing sternly throughout the subterranean tunnels. 'Come forth and meet death at the point of my sword.'

Greenskin blood swathed the captain's noble face, drying slowly and forming a crust that reminded Scipio of the tribal markings of their forebears from the earliest days of Macragge.

They had been searching the darkness of the cave system for almost an hour, but as yet their quarry had not been sighted. Orks lay in ambush – those that had managed to elude Arcus Helios's vanguard of Terminators – waiting with blades and guns behind corners and in pitch-black alcoves. The auto-senses of the Astartes alerted them to every danger. Their blood was up, and the greenskins were cut down before they got a chance to move.

Scipio probed the blackness just behind the captain and his Lions, Iulus alongside him. The sergeant was tight-lipped and tense as he panned his bolt pistol slowly across the width of the tunnel. Behind them the rest of the Immortals brought up the rear, dousing secondary tunnels with bursts of promethium from their flamer to burn out any potential ambushers.

Scipio felt the collective agitation rising amongst his brothers and knew that none felt it more keenly than Sicarius. The longer Zanzag evaded them, the greater the chance the ork warlord would escape their wrath completely.

A crackle from the comm-feed on the open channel released the tension.

It was Sergeant Octavian. 'Brother-Captain, Squad Helios is reporting sunlight from the opposite side of the caves, five hundred metres west of your position, and they have found a passage wide enough for Brother Ultracius to negotiate.'

'Muster the battle group,' ordered Sicarius, breaking into a run. 'Do it at once.'

Sunlight streamed in through the wide cleft in the tunnel wall. Sicarius stalked out and was bathed in the glorious daylight beyond. His armour gleamed despite the blood, his sword blade shimmering with captured fire.

The captain had caught up with Squad Helios swiftly, the Terminators, who were ideally suited to the rigours of tunnel fighting, having ventured ahead. Arcus Helios and his warriors arrayed themselves around Sicarius and his Lions as the High Suzerain emerged from the caves.

Scipio was barely through the breach in the wall with Iulus when the bestial cries of greenskins filled the air.

Zanzag was here with the remnants of his shattered force. The orks had gathered at the summit of a sloping, steep-sided ravine, baring their tusks and bellowing defiance. All his cunning, the tricks and the decoys had failed the warlord; now all he had left was brute force. In a final gambit, he charged the Ultramarines vanguard, intent on taking down its leader.

'Ultramarines, engage and destroy!' roared Sicarius.

A brief volley of bolter fire staggered the mob of

scar-veterans surging forward with their warlord, before blades were drawn and the battle became close and dirty.

A metallic scream of pain hammered Scipio's senses, and from the corner of his eye he saw a Terminator from Squad Helios fall, slain by Zanzag's power claw. The massive warlord stepped over the corpse, grinning madly as he closed on Sicarius.

The captain rushed in, Tempest Blade upraised, Guilliman's name on his lips.

The battle rushed by in a blur of blood, steel and smoke. Acrid burning flesh filled Scipio's nose as he fought side-by-side with Iulus; Ultracius venting his flamer to their flank. The dreadnought stomped forward, crushing the still-burning ork carcasses, before unleashing its assault cannon.

Greenskins were mown down with terrible bursts of fire, chewed apart in their armour. Together with the fury of Arcus Helios and his warriors, smashing the scar-veterans apart with their power fists in retribution for their dead battle-brother, the dreadnought had gouged a clearing in the horde.

Scipio took a moment in the brief lull to gather his bearings. One sight dominated all: Sicarius fighting the ork warlord at the ravine's peak.

Lightning cracked overhead, and thunder rippled downward as a dry storm broke in the heavens as if in empathy of the titanic struggle unfolding below.

Astartes purity and courage matched against greenskin brutality and savagery. One must break before the battle was done.

Iulus stormed up the incline in support of his

captain and Scipio followed him, bolt pistol screaming. Through the melee, he saw the crackling energy of
the Tempest Blade as Sicarius rained blows like chained
lightning upon his foe. Zanzag replied, battering the
captain's defences mercilessly with his power claw.

In the end, willpower proved the deciding factor.

Scipio had overtaken Iulus, tearing through the
greenskins with brutal efficiency. His fellow sergeant
was just behind him when Scipio saw Sicarius cut
Zanzag's power claw off at the shoulder. It was a
mammoth blow, two-handed, and left the captain
open to a counter. But the attack didn't come. Zanzag staggered, dark blood gushing from the ruined
stump of the partly cauterised wound.

Sicarius stepped in close. 'I've already killed you
once, beast,' he spat. 'This time I'll make it stick.'

He rammed the Tempest Blade through the creature's eye-socket and impaled its bestial skull with a
grunt of effort. Withdrawing the blood-slick sword,
Sicarius watched Zanzag keel over and lie still in the
sun-scorched sand.

The captain's victory proved decisive. As happened
at the stronghold, the greenskins lost all heart with
the death of their leader. What paltry ork forces
remained were quickly rounded up by the Space
Marines and slaughtered. Sicarius took no further
part in the combat. He merely stood atop the summit
of the ravine and raised his bloodied sword in salute.

The Ultramarines cheered as one, raising weapons
aloft. Scipio added his voice to the belligerent chorus and exhaled with relief.

Zanzag was dead at last. Black Reach had been saved.

* * *

The cavern was destroyed. Copious amounts of charges were rigged throughout and threaded along the tunnel complex beyond. Any greenskins that might still have been lurking inside would be buried alive under tons of rubble.

Sicarius even instructed the *Valin's Revenge* to bombard the site thoroughly with plasma torpedoes in order to be certain. In a strange way, seeing those deadly falling stars, it was as if the campaign had come full circle.

It had been a great victory, one that would be retold time and again from the prestigious annals of Ultramarines' military history. But it was not without cost. Many battle-brothers had lost their lives to the green tide, and their laurels would array the honour wall back on the strike cruiser. It would take a little time to replenish the dead, though Apothecary Venatio had performed his duty well and no warrior slain would go into the halls of honour without his gene-seed paving the way for a successor for the Chapter. Many amongst the 10th, the brave-hearted scouts who had infiltrated the warlord's lair with Brother-Sergeant Telion, would earn their black carapace for their part in the campaign and become full battle-brothers.

With the death of Zanzag, the orks had capitulated. Other warlords, seeking to exploit the power void, had stepped forward only to be crushed by a relentless Sicarius in a series of punitive strikes against the remaining greenskins. His wrath had been swift and merciless. In three short, blood-filled days, the orks had been all but scoured from the planet and the

Ultramarines were recalled to the *Valin's Revenge*, leaving the Sable Gunners to reclaim the rest of Black Reach from the scattered ork forces that still remained.

Scipio was kneeling in the strike cruiser's reclusiam, head bowed in reverence with his bolter laid out before him. It was good to be clad in his power armour again, to feel its heft. Re-sanctified by Chaplain Orad, the MkVII suit was part of him, a venerable ally. Scipio had missed it.

'Seeking solace, brother?' a voice asked, echoing through the darkness.

'Solace seems in short supply whenever I venture to the reclusiam,' Scipio answered. 'I am thinking perhaps it should be renamed the colloquium. Either that or I will perform supplications on the engineering deck with the serfs.'

Iulus's laughter betrayed his position as he approached through the shadows.

'My apologies, brother,' he said sincerely, his face cast in the light of votive candles. Iulus looked to the honour wall where Scipio was genuflecting. Gilded laurels, awards for valour, were pinioned there in remembrance of those who had fallen on Black Reach.

The granite in his expression softened slightly with a sudden change in mood. 'A prayer for battles won?'

'For brothers lost,' Scipio replied. 'My benedictions are done, anyway,' he added, getting to his feet. 'What news of the company? Have you seen much of Praxor since our return to the ship?'

'He is engrossed in battle drills and training. I don't think he has left the gymnasia for six straight days.'

'The duelling cages will be broken into submission by the time we visit them again,' Scipio remarked, following Iulus as he led them out of the reclusiam. 'He still feels slighted,' he asserted, once they were in the corridor beyond.

'Perhaps...' Iulus replied. 'But then Praxor Manorian has always favoured glory over duty.'

'And what or whom do you favour, brother?' asked Scipio.

Iulus's face darkened. 'I was wrong,' he admitted. 'Whether or not our captain seeks the right hand of Calgar over Agemman, I do not know. In truth, I no longer care. I favour the Chapter and it alone. I witnessed a hero wrest Black Reach from those xenos scum. A hero, Scipio.' Iulus stopped and faced him, briefly blocking Scipio's view into the reclusiam. 'To besmirch his name, however meant, is at odds with that. Black Reach will be forever remembered. It will go down in history as a great victory.'

Scipio maintained his silence.

'You think differently?' ventured Iulus.

Scipio could see past the sergeant's shoulder and back through the reclusiam's arch. His gaze fell upon the many laurels on the honour wall, the posthumous medals awarded to the dead. Hekor's name, as well as many others, was amongst them.

Scipio's face hardened. 'No. It was a great victory, brother.'

ABOUT THE AUTHOR

Nick Kyme is the author of the Horus Heresy novels *Deathfire*, *Vulkan Lives*, *Old Earth* and *Sons of the Forge*, the novellas *Promethean Sun* and *Scorched Earth*, and the audio dramas *Censure* and *Red Marked*. His novella *Feat of Iron* was a *New York Times* bestseller in the Horus Heresy collection, *The Primarchs*. Nick is well known for his popular Salamanders novels, including *Rebirth*, the Space Marine Battles novel *Damnos*, and numerous short stories. He has also written fiction set in the world of Warhammer, most notably the Warhammer Chronicles novel *The Great Betrayal* and the Age of Sigmar story 'Borne by the Storm', included in the novel *Warstorm*. He lives and works in Nottingham, and has a rabbit.

DARK IMPERIUM
Guy Haley

The galaxy has changed. Darkness spreads, warp storms split reality and Chaos is everywhere – even Ultramar. As Roboute Guilliman's Indomitus Crusade draws to a close, he must brave the perils of the warp to reach his home and save it from the depredations of the Plague God.

An extract from
Dark Imperium

'My Lord Guilliman! Your veterans await your command,' said Andros, his voice ringing from the voxmitter set below his helm.

'We stand prepared, my primarch,' said Aeonid Thiel. His voice, rich and soft, was unmoderated by machinery. It was not so very long after the Heresy, and Thiel was still young for a Space Marine, though his face was lined with cares.

Guilliman looked down upon his captains resolutely. The primarch overtopped even Andros in his massive Terminator armour. He was a living god, humanity's might captured and moulded as flesh.

Thiel gazed back, seemingly unable to take his eyes from the face of his gene-sire. Thiel was a good warrior, tested in battle many times, unafraid to voice his mind and modest enough to hide the love he had for his lord, but it shone in his face like a light.

Such devotion they bear me, thought Guilliman, *even as I fail them.*

There were so few of his original Legion left alive, and their replacements were born of a different, less certain era. Thiel's regard was tempered by long friendship, and he had never lost his rebellious streak. The younger Space Marines were another matter. Guilliman remembered when his warriors had been less reverent. They had been better times.

'We depart immediately,' he said, his voice uncompromising. 'The traitor will not escape again. The warriors of six Chapters stand ready to aid us. We shall not fail. To your stations – prepare for mass teleport.'

'My lord, we are prepared,' said Andros carefully. 'But the enemy will outnumber us greatly. I am concerned for our chances of success. What is the practical action should resistance prove overwhelming? It is Second Captain Thiel's and my opinion that you should remain here. We shall occupy the enemy, while the *Gauntlet of Power* withdraws. We cannot–'

The Avenging Son cut Andros dead with a look.

'Too much blood has been shed on my behalf. I will not shy from this fight,' Guilliman said, and his tone would brook no disagreement. 'There can be no retreat until the *Pride of the Emperor* is crippled. I must face my brother and occupy him while these tasks are done. And if I must fight him, I will kill him, or I will die in the attempt. I cannot let him escape unpunished again. My sons,' he added, his voice softening, 'it is the only way to escape this trap.'

Andros bowed his helmeted head. Thiel paused

a moment, uncertain, before doing the same. Sure of their agreement, Guilliman took his own helm from a grav-platform pushed by two mortal men. He mounted the teleport platform – stepping directly onto it with no need of the steps that led from the deck – and turned to address his sons.

'Now, my warriors, let us show my brother the consequences of turning upon the Imperium of Terra!'

'We march for Macragge!' they bellowed, and their combined voices were enough to drown out the thunder of battle.

Guilliman's Invictus Suzerain guard followed him onto the teleport pad. They formed a protective ring around him, their shields and power axes held up in a shield wall in preparation for teleportation directly into the jaws of battle.

To those around him, Guilliman was an infallible leader, his abilities supernatural. Even to the rational Ultramarines, who believed the Emperor of Mankind to be a man and not a god, and likewise His primarch sons, a sense of near-religious awe had crept into their attitude towards him. It had only become more pronounced since the last days of the Heresy.

But Roboute Guilliman was not infallible.

He knew this course of action to be fraught with risk. Andros had been right to raise the possibility of defeat. The primarch only wished he could praise his son for his insight rather than dismissing his concerns. His campaign against the Emperor's Children had, to all purposes, failed. Fulgrim had the initiative. Guilliman's choices had been made for him.

The pieces were set on the board, there was only one option: they had to withdraw.

Currently, withdrawal was impossible. If the *Gauntlet of Power* broke off from the fight, then the *Pride of the Emperor* would inflict massive damage upon the battle-barge. Fulgrim would then most likely attempt a boarding assault of his own once their defences were shattered. Guilliman could not allow his brother to do that at a time of his choosing.

The primarch's powerful mind had examined all possibilities. His own strategic treatises would have him retreat quickly, forming a fighting rearguard so that he might withdraw those of his ships that he could, minimising the damage to his flagship by sacrificing many of his others. Expending the lives of other men to save his own was not to Guilliman's liking, especially when he saw a slim chance for true victory. He could not ignore this opportunity to slay his treacherous sibling. Guilliman had come to the conclusion that by defying his own tactical orthodoxies, he might surprise Fulgrim.

It was a slender chance. Fulgrim might well have dropped his ship's shields on purpose, a mocking re-enactment of Horus' last gambit to lure the Emperor aboard his ship at the end of the siege of Terra.

Guilliman had his own plans. Several boarding forces with independent but mutually supportive objectives would teleport in simultaneously with his own force. Teams drawn from multiple Chapters were tasked to head for the enginarium, the command deck, the navigatorium, the magazine, the subsidiary command deck and the main gunnery control. If only half of his strike teams were successful, they had a good chance of crippling the *Pride of the Emperor* from within. His warriors had orders to withdraw immediately once their objectives had been achieved. He would make sure as many survived as possible; he would not let his sons pay the price for his mistakes.

He had to settle the reckoning for his own errors.

Guilliman could not deny he had been hooked and played like a fish. All he could do was struggle free and bite the one who had snared him.

'Make ready! We go to war!' he called.

At his signal, the machines of the teleport deck hummed into life. Giant reaction columns crackled with immense power, feeding the focusing arrays that would tear open the veil between real space and the warp. They glowed with painful light. As they shone brighter, curls of materialising corposant were leached from initiation prongs and fed into containment flasks, where it twisted as if alive.

So many of my brothers are dead, fallen to Chaos or lost, thought Guilliman. *We assumed we were immortal. We are not. My time must come, but not today. Not at the hands of Fulgrim.*

The arcane machineries of teleportation whooped and hummed, the deck vibrating with their activity. The tumult built to a crescendo.

A booming crack and flash of actinic light whited out the teleport deck. Suppressant vapours gushed from wide-mouthed tubes in anticipation of fires from over-stressed machinery. Human armsmen raised their shotguns in case of warp breach and daemonic incursion.

None came. Signal strobes blinked: red, red, red, then blue.

'Teleport success, teleport success,' droned a mechanical voice.

The lumens came back on. Corposant flasks emptied to the sounds of half-formed screams. Atmospheric vents drew smoke away, revealing empty pads. Adepts consulted vid screens and paper cogitator strips, and relief crossed their faces at the readouts.

Roboute Guilliman and his warriors were aboard the *Pride of the Emperor.*